Clint walke{...} look in windows. The house wasn't that big. {...} was in the back, and when he peered in a window he saw a man lying on the floor.

"Sheriff! Back here!"

The sheriff came running from the other direction. Clint pointed in the window.

"What do you say now?" he asked.

"I say we better get in there," Coffey said. "Come on, we'll force the front door."

Together they ran to the front of the house. The sheriff attacked the door with his bulk and it slammed open. They ran to the back and looked down at the body.

"Who is it?" Clint asked.

"It's him," Coffey said. "It's Reardon."

"Damn!" Clint said.

THE GUNSMITH

363

THE DEATH LIST

J. R. ROBERTS

JOVE BOOKS, NEW YORK

THE BERKLEY PUBLISHING GROUP
Published by the Penguin Group
Penguin Group (USA) Inc.
375 Hudson Street, New York, New York 10014, USA
Penguin Group (Canada), 90 Eglinton Avenue East, Suite 700, Toronto, Ontario M4P 2Y3, Canada
(a division of Pearson Penguin Canada Inc.)
Penguin Books Ltd., 80 Strand, London WC2R 0RL, England
Penguin Group Ireland, 25 St. Stephen's Green, Dublin 2, Ireland (a division of Penguin Books Ltd.)
Penguin Group (Australia), 250 Camberwell Road, Camberwell, Victoria 3124, Australia
(a division of Pearson Australia Group Pty. Ltd.)
Penguin Books India Pvt. Ltd., 11 Community Centre, Panchsheel Park, New Delhi—110 017, India
Penguin Group (NZ), 67 Apollo Drive, Rosedale, Auckland 0632, New Zealand
(a division of Pearson New Zealand Ltd.)
Penguin Books (South Africa) (Pty.) Ltd., 24 Sturdee Avenue, Rosebank, Johannesburg 2196,
South Africa

Penguin Books Ltd., Registered Offices: 80 Strand, London WC2R 0RL, England

This is a work of fiction. Names, characters, places, and incidents either are the product of the author's imagination or are used fictitiously, and any resemblance to actual persons, living or dead, business establishments, events, or locales is entirely coincidental

THE DEATH LIST

A Jove Book / published by arrangement with the author

PRINTING HISTORY
Jove edition / March 2012

Copyright © 2012 by Robert J. Randisi.
Cover illustration by Sergio Giovine.

ISBN: 978-0-515-15049-0

JOVE®
Jove Books are published by The Berkley Publishing Group,
a division of Penguin Group (USA) Inc.,
375 Hudson Street, New York, New York 10014.
JOVE® is a registered trademark of Penguin Group (USA) Inc.
The "J" design is a trademark of Penguin Group (USA) Inc.

PRINTED IN THE UNITED STATES OF AMERICA

10 9 8 7 6 5 4 3 2 1

ONE

Clint was in the livery stable in Labyrinth, Texas, working on Eclipse's coat with a brush, when the telegraph key operator found him.

"Hey, Mr. Adams," the man said. "They tol' me over to Rick's Place that you was here."

"Hello, Chet," Clint said. "What've you got there?"

"Telegram for ya," Chet said, handing it over.

Clint turned to face the tall, gangly young man.

"You could have left it with Rick."

"He weren't available," Chet said, "and besides, I thought it might be important."

"Okay," Clint said, "thanks."

Chet handed the telegram over. Clint did not offer the young man a tip, because Chet always refused. They'd finally gotten to this point, where Clint did not even offer.

"I hope it ain't bad news," Chet said. "I gotta get back to work."

"I'll be seeing you," Clint said. He was only halfway finished with Eclipse's grooming, and did not want to read a telegram at the moment—especially if it had bad news. So he folded it, put it in his shirt pocket, and went back to combing some tangles out of the big Darley Arabian's mane.

Later, Clint was in Rick's Place—owned and run by his friend, Rick Hartman—having a beer and talking with the new bartender, Elroy.

Elroy was a young man who had been hired while Clint was away for a few weeks, and was now thrilled to be serving beer to the Gunsmith.

"They tol' me when I took this job that you spent a lot of time in this town," he said.

"I do," Clint said, "it's just that lately things have been keeping me on the trail."

"Well, I hope you're back for a while, Mr. Adams," Elroy said. "Excuse me."

He moved down the bar either to serve some new customers, or because his boss, Rick Hartman, was approaching.

"Is he botherin' you?" Rick asked.

"No," Clint said, "he's okay."

"I'm not so sure," Rick said. "I might have to fire him."

"How long's he been working here?" Clint asked.

"A few weeks."

"And you're going to fire him already?"

"He's not doing the job," Rick said. "For instance, did he tell you the telegraph operator was here with a telegram for you?"

Clint slapped his forehead with his palm.

"I forgot about that. Chet said he came here and was sent to the livery."

"Well," Rick said, somewhat mollified, "at least he didn't forget that. What was it about? Somebody lookin' for help again?"

"I don't know," Clint said, taking the telegram from his pocket. "I forgot to read it."

"You must've been workin' on Eclipse," Rick said. "That horse is the only thing that could make you forget to read a telegram—that and a woman."

"It was Eclipse," Clint said, "but I'll read it right now."

He unfolded the yellow flimsy, read it, frowning.

"What's goin' on?" Rick asked.

"This is odd," Clint said. "All it says is that there should be an envelope over at the post office in General Delivery for me by now."

"That's it?"

Clint handed it over. Rick looked at it, and also frowned.

"If the post office has an envelope for you, why haven't they delivered it?"

"I don't know," Clint said, taking the telegram back. "Maybe they specifically want me to go over and ask for it."

"I don't get it," Rick said.

"I don't either," Clint said, "so I guess I'll go and get it, and then we'll both know what it's about."

"Want me to go with you?"

"What for?"

"To watch your back."

"At the post office?" Clint asked.

Rick shrugged and said, "You never know."

Clint said, "Hey, suit yourself. I'm heading over there right now."

"Lead the way," Rick said.

TWO

The post office had opened in Labyrinth, Texas, just a few months ago. That made the postmaster fairly new in town, but he did most of his drinking and gambling in Rick's Place.

"Hey, Rick," John Luke said as Clint and Rick entered. "What brings you here? Expecting a letter?"

Luke was in his forties, had been a postmaster in the East before being assigned to this post.

"I'm not, but my friend is. I don't think you've met Clint Adams yet."

"Mr. Adams," Luke said. "Well, this is a pleasure. I've heard a lot about you since I arrived here in town."

"It's good to meet you," Clint said, shaking hands with the man.

"So you're the one expecting a letter?" Luke asked.

"A letter, an envelope," Clint said. "Something. It should have been sent care of General Delivery."

"Ah," Luke said, "very good. I'll have a look."

Luke disappeared and then returned with a white envelope.

"This looks like it," he said, handing it to Clint.

On the front was written "Clint Adams, General Delivery, Labyrinth, Texas."

"Looks like it," Clint said. "Thanks."

"See you, Luke," Rick said, and the two friends left the post office.

They went to Rick's Place, which, this early, was almost empty. When Elroy saw them come in, he said, "Finally, some business."

"Two beers," Rick said, and then added, "on the house."

"Fine with me," Elroy said, "gives me somethin' to do anyway."

They took the beers to a table in the back, where Rick usually sat.

"You gonna open that?" Rick asked.

"I thought I might," Clint said.

"What kind of trouble do you think is in that envelope?"

"What makes you think it's not somebody inviting me to a wedding?"

"Not you," Rick said. "Trouble finds you."

"Let's see."

Clint opened the envelope, took out two pieces of paper.

"Two letters?"

"One letter," Clint said, "and a list."

"What kind of list?"

"I don't know," Clint said, looking it over, "it's a list of names."

"Names of what?"

"Men," Clint said. "Looks like . . . ten names, with a location next to each one."

"Lemme see."

Clint handed the list across the table to Rick, then looked at the letter.

"I don't know any of these names," Rick said. "What's this about?"

"Listen to this," Clint said. "The letter is unsigned, but it's from someone who says he's going to kill each of these ten people and he challenges me to stop him."

"See what I mean?" Rick asked. "Trouble. Why you?"

"It doesn't say."

"Well," Rick said, looking at the list again, "all you've got to do is send a telegram to each of these people and warn them."

"No, no," Clint said, "the letter goes on to say I have to do it in person."

"Or else what?"

"Apparently he plans to kill them in order," Clint said. "If I should try to notify them without going to each city or town, he will kill them out of order. He says I'll have no idea which one he's going to kill next."

"What do you care? Notify the law in each of those places and forget about it."

"Because at the end he says that when all ten of them are dead, I'll know that it was my fault."

"That's bull," Rick said. "Some nut sends you a list and a letter, and you're gonna believe him?"

"Can I afford not to believe him?" Clint asked, taking the list back from Rick.

"I say yes, you can."

"I don't know . . ."

"When is this supposed to start?"

Clint looked at the letter again.

"It doesn't say. No date. I guess it started when I opened this letter."

"Okay, who's first, and where?"

"The name is William Reardon, and he lives in Vega, Texas."

"Well," Rick said, "at least the first one is easy to get to."

"That's way north," Clint said.

"Still closer, right?"

"Right."

Clint stood up.

"What are you doing?" Rick asked.

"I've got to get moving right away," Clint said, "if I'm going to make it to Vega in time to save Mr. Reardon's life."

"And if you go there and he's in no danger?"

"Well, then we'll know the whole thing was a hoax, won't we?"

"When are you gonna ride out?" Rick asked as Clint headed for the door.

"As soon as I saddle up!"

THREE

Vega was a small Texas town about ten miles west of Amarillo. When Clint rode in, he went right to the sheriff's office. He'd been in the saddle for a little under six hundred miles. He needed a steak, a beer, and a bed, but first he needed information.

He entered the office, found a deputy sitting behind a desk.

"I'm looking for the sheriff," he said.

The deputy, in his twenties, looked up at Clint and said, "Who are you?"

"I'm the man asking for the sheriff. It's very important I talk to him right away."

The young man stood up, puffed out his chest, and hitched up his gun belt.

"Well, he ain't here and I'm in charge—"

Had he not been in the saddle so long, Clint's temper might not have been so short.

He closed on the deputy, put his hand on his chest, grabbed his badge, and pushed him back down into his

chair. Then he ground the badge against his chest so that
the pin pierced the flesh.

"Ow!"

"I'm not going to ask you again," Clint said. "Where's
the sheriff?"

"Down the street in Ma's Café havin' lunch," the
young deputy blurted out.

Clint released his hold on the badge, turned, and left
the office.

As he entered Ma's Café, the smell of burning meat hit
him and his stomach grumbled. There were several tables
taken. Near the back he saw a man with a badge, a shock
of gray hair, and a heavily lined face eating a steak. He
walked to the table.

"Sheriff?"

"That's right," the man said, "but I'm eatin'."

"Your deputy told me where to find you."

"Then he's fired."

"My name is Clint Adams."

The sheriff stopped with his fork halfway to his mouth
and looked up at Clint.

"You on the level?"

"I am."

The lawman put his fork down and sat back in his
chair.

"Just get to town?"

"A minute ago."

"Have a seat," the man said.

"I really don't have time for that," Clint said. "I'm
looking for a man named Reardon, William Reardon."

"Bill Reardon."

"You know him?"

"I do, yeah."

"I have reason to believe his life is in danger."

"From you?"

"No."

"Then who?"

"I don't know that."

"Then how do you know he's in danger?"

"Look," Clint said, "if you can take me to him, I'll explain on the way."

The sheriff looked down at his steak. Clint looked at it, too. It was too well done for him, but he could have made an exception at that moment.

"When did you eat last?" the sheriff asked.

"Miles and miles back."

"Ma!" he yelled.

An older woman came out of the kitchen, drying her hands on her apron.

"Yeah, whataya want, Ray?"

"I need you to put this steak on two pieces of bread for me."

"It's called a sandwich, Ray."

"I know it," Ray said, standing up. "And make another one for this man. We'll be eatin' in the saddle."

"This some sort of emergency?" she asked.

"That's right."

She nodded and said, "Comin' up."

"Let's walk outside," the sheriff said, grabbing his hat.

They stepped out the door and waited.

"She won't take long."

"What's your name?" Clint asked.

"Ray Coffey," the lawman said.

"Why do you call her ma?"

"Rest of the town calls her that because that's what she named this place," Coffey said.

"And you?"

"I got another reason," he said. "She's my ma."

Clint stared at the man closely.

"How old are you?" he asked.

"Me? I'm sixty."

FOUR

Sheriff Coffey told Clint that Bill Reardon had a ranch outside of town. Along the way Clint told Reardon about the telegram, the letter, and the list.

"That sounds crazy," Coffey said.

"Yeah, it does."

"But you came all this way on the basis of this letter and list?"

"I couldn't take the chance," Clint said. "I'm hoping this visit will tell me something, though."

"Like what?"

"Maybe Mr. Reardon has some idea who'd like to kill him," Clint said. "And maybe he will recognize some of the other names on the list."

"Well, I sure didn't," Coffey said. "Never heard of any of those people."

"Neither have I."

"How many were there?"

"Ten."

"I was thinkin' maybe they was a jury, but not ten."

"Maybe two others have already died," Clint said. "I had that thought. Reardon can tell us if he ever served on a jury with these people. It's doubtful, though. I mean, they live all over the country."

"And you're gonna ride all over the country to try an' save 'em?"

"I guess that'll depend on what we find out from Mr. Reardon."

Reardon's ranch was only a couple of hours outside of town. They had finished their steak sandwiches long before they got there, and Clint thanked Coffey for the thought.

"You looked hungry."

When they arrived, they reined in outside and dismounted.

"Place looks empty," Clint said. "Where are the hands?"

"There are none," Coffey said. "Used to be, but Bill's fallen on hard times, had to let everybody go."

"When did that happen?" Clint asked.

"Over the past few years."

They walked up to the door of the small main house and the sheriff knocked. Clint saw a bunkhouse, a barn, and a corral in a state of disrepair.

"Bill!" Coffey shouted, banging on the door. "Come on, man, it's Sheriff Coffey."

Still no answer.

"We've got to go in," Clint said.

"No, wait a second," Coffey said, putting his hand on Clint's chest, "we can't just go bustin' in on a man's home."

"What do you want to do?"

"Let's walk around the house, look in the windows, see what we can see."

"Yeah, okay," Clint said. "I'll go this way . . ."

They split up.

Clint walked around the left side of the house, stopping to look in windows. The house wasn't that big. Before long he was in the back, and when he peered in a window, he saw a man lying on the floor.

"Sheriff! Back here!"

The sheriff came running from the other direction. Clint pointed in the window.

"What do you say now?" he asked.

"I say we better get in there," Coffey said. "Come on, we'll force the front door."

Together they ran to the front of the house. The sheriff attacked the door with his bulk and it slammed open. They ran to the back and looked down at the body.

"Who is it?" Clint asked.

"It's him," Coffey said. "It's Reardon."

"Damn!" Clint said.

FIVE

"Take a look," Coffey said.

Clint knelt down, moved the body, found the bullet hole—in the back. He stood up.

"I'm too late."

"Could be a coincidence," Coffey said.

"I don't believe in them."

"We better go back to town, send the undertaker back with my deputy."

Clint nodded. They left the house.

"Mind if I have a look around first?" Clint asked.

"Go ahead," Coffey said, mounting up. "Come and see me when you get back to town."

"Okay."

The sheriff rode off and Clint walked around the place, trailing Eclipse behind him. He checked the bunkhouse, and the barn, went to have a look at the corral.

When he was done, he walked back to the house and went inside, dropping Eclipse's reins to the ground.

He went to the body again. This time he went through

the dead man's pockets, found nothing. What did he expect to find? Maybe a note from his letter sender?

He went through the rest of the house, stopped at Reardon's desk, went through the drawers. He found some unpaid bills, but nothing else.

He went back out to his horse, looked around. Whoever had killed Reardon hadn't left anything behind. He wondered if the letter writer had done it himself, or had sent someone to have it done?

Did he mean to send Clint scurrying all over the country, while he himself simply used a different killer in each place? If that was the case, there was no way he could save any of them.

And if there was no way to save any of them, then why try?

He mounted up and rode toward town.

When he got back to Vega, he rode to the sheriff's office. He still had to get himself a room at a hotel, and get Eclipse taken care of.

He entered the office and Coffey looked up at him.

"You pass them on the road?" the man asked.

"Yeah," Clint said. "The undertaker and your deputy."

"My deputy was kinda mad at you," Coffey said.

"I guess I sort of insisted he tell me where you were," Clint said. "I'll apologize."

Clint sat across from the sheriff.

"Coffee?"

Clint hesitated, then said, "Sure."

The lawman poured two cups and handed Clint one.

"You can call me Ray," he said, "just to avoid confusion."

"Thanks."

The sheriff sat back down behind his desk.

"What are you gonna do now?"

"Get a room, get some sleep," Clint said, "and then move on to the next one."

"Where will that be?"

Clint took the list from his pocket and checked it.

"Kansas."

"What's the name?"

"Dave Britton."

"Never heard of him."

"Me neither."

"Why don't you send a telegram—oh, wait, yeah, you said."

"Right."

"You find anything out there?"

"No," Clint said, "nothing."

"Did you think he'd leave a note?"

"It occurred to me."

"Maybe he left one at the hotel."

"How many hotels in town?"

"One," Coffey said.

"Then maybe there is a note there."

"A man like that," Coffey said, "would want to gloat, don't you think?"

"Yeah," Clint said. "I do."

Clint finished his coffee and set the empty cup on the desk.

"Thanks. Good coffee."

"Nobody's ever told me that before."

Clint stood up.

"I'll take care of my horse and get a room. I'll leave early in the morning."

"You want a real steak dinner?" Coffey asked.

"Oh, yeah."

"I'll meet you in the lobby of the hotel in an hour," the lawman said.

"Thanks," Clint said.

He left the sheriff's office and walked Eclipse to the livery stable.

SIX

When he got to the hotel and checked in, the clerk said, "There's a note here for you, Mr. Adams."

"I thought there might be. Thanks."

He carried the note up to his room and sat on the bed to read it.

"Too late," it said, "and in case you're wondering, I did it myself. And I'll keep doing it until you stop me."

That was it. Everything was spelled correctly, and the handwriting was almost elegant.

He folded it and put it in his pocket with the list.

There was water in a pitcher on the dresser, and a chipped basin. He poured some of the water into the basin and washed up. His stomach grumbled. The sandwich had staved off hunger to some extent, but now it was back full force. A steak dinner sounded great to him. He decided to count on that, and think about the death list later that night—or maybe in the morning.

He went down to the lobby to wait for the sheriff.

* * *

"I'm surprised a town this small has two restaurants where the food is edible."

"Ma's is edible," the sheriff said. "This place has good steak dinners."

They each ordered one. When it came and Clint tasted the food, he told Sheriff Coffey he was right.

"This is good."

"They do a steak and eggs in the morning, too, if you're interested," Coffey said. "And they open early."

"I'll remember," Clint said. "You get Reardon's body to the undertaker's?"

"Yep."

"Find anything I should know about?"

"Nothin'," Coffey said. "Shot once in the back. Nothin' unusual."

Clint nodded, chewed some potatoes.

"What are your plans?"

"The same," Clint said. "I'll head out tomorrow, ride to Kansas, see what I can do there. I'm behind, and wondering if I'll always be behind."

"And you can't jump ahead a name?"

Clint didn't answer right away. He cut a chunk of steak, and chewed it while he gave the question some thought.

"If I jump ahead, I'll be giving up a life in Kansas," he said.

"But if that man is already dead, you might be getting a head start on the next one. Where's that?"

Clint took out the list.

"Tennessee."

"Same direction," Coffey said. "If you send a telegram

to Kansas, find out whether or not that man is dead or alive—"

"The letter writer warned me against sending telegrams."

"How would he know?"

"I don't know," Clint said, "but can I take the chance?"

They ate for a while, alone with their thoughts, before the sheriff spoke.

"What if I send a telegram?" he asked. "Get the information for you?"

"If a telegram comes in with the name of the next man, it might not matter who is sending it. No, for now I'll just have to head to Kansas and see what I find when I get there."

"Then it doesn't seem like I can be much help at all," Coffey said.

"Maybe not, but I appreciate the offer," Clint said.

Coffey walked Clint back to his hotel. It was quiet on the street.

"Always this quiet?" he asked.

"Just when the Gunsmith is in town," Coffey said.

"Word got around?"

Coffey shrugged.

"It is a small town."

"Guess I shouldn't stop off in the saloon, then."

"You could stop for a beer."

"Nah," Clint said. "I'm going to my room to get some rest. I've got to get going early."

"Don't know that I'll see you before you leave, then," Coffey said as they got to the door of the hotel. He extended his hand. "I wish you luck."

Clint shook the man's hand.

"I appreciate your help."

The sheriff walked away and Clint entered the hotel and went to his room.

SEVEN

Clint rose very early the next morning, found that Coffey had been right. The restaurant opened very early, even before it was fully light. He saddled Eclipse, left him outside, and went in for a steak-and-eggs breakfast.

He read the list again while he ate, and the note that had been left at the hotel. Also the letter that had accompanied the list. They all seemed to have been written by the same hand. That meant whoever had mailed the letter and list had been in Vega to write the note. He was going to have to go on the assumption that the same man was doing the killing. With that assumption, it became clear that the man was ahead of him.

He finished his breakfast but, before leaving town, went back to the livery.

"Problem?" the liveryman asked.

"No, just a question. Any other strangers come to town in the last few days? Leave their horse here?"

"Nope," the man said. "Ain't nobody been here all week 'cept you."

"Thanks."

He left the livery, went back to the hotel, and asked the clerk the same question.

"No, sir," the clerk said, showing him the register, "ain't had no strangers all week 'ceptin' you."

"Okay, thanks."

He mounted up and left town.

That night, over a campfire, Clint pondered the results of his ride to Vega.

The killer didn't put his horse up in the livery, didn't register at the hotel. But he managed to kill William Reardon. So he came to Vegas knowing what he wanted to do. He went directly to Reardon's ranch, killed him, and moved on. Nobody saw him.

That being the case, he was a good day—maybe more—ahead of Clint. The only way he could close that distance between them was to push Eclipse—hard. But he didn't want to burn the big Darley Arabian out.

He took the list out of his pocket. Instead of looking at the names, he looked at the locations. Kansas, Tennessee, Colorado (Denver), Minnesota, Saint Louis . . . there was no rhyme or reason to the order. He was riding Clint all over the country. Tennessee to Denver would be a hell of a ride. He wondered about leaving Eclipse somewhere and using the railroad. Would that get him where he was going on time? Was the killer riding everywhere? Or was he using other modes of transportation as well?

Maybe a train trip from Kansas to Tennessee might answer a few questions, but first he had to get to Kansas.

* * *

Clint rode into Dexter, Kansas, in the afternoon. A small town, but twice the size of Vega. How was the killer picking his victims? Did they all live in small towns? Was that the point?

He headed straight for the sheriff's office. He was going to have to repeat this process each place he went.

Or was he?

Maybe it would make sense to change his method of operation sooner rather than later.

Instead of riding to the sheriff's office, he went looking for the undertaker.

The undertaker was on Main Street. Outside was a shingle that said, JEDEDIAH BLEMISH, UNDERTAKER.

Clint entered.

"Hello?" he said to the empty front room.

"Hello!" came a response from the back. A curtain was pulled back and a strange-looking man appeared. He was barely five foot two, probably didn't weigh a hundred pounds with a pocket full of rice.

"Can I help you?"

"Are you Blemish?"

"That's me," the man said. He appeared to be in his thirties, with a shock of red hair that almost stood up on end. He extended his hand and Clint shook it. It felt like the hand of a child.

"And who are you?"

"My name is Clint Adams."

Blemish pulled his hand back.

"The Gunsmith?"

"That's right."

"You've made a lot of work for those in my profession," Blemish said.

"Probably not as much as you've heard."

"Hmm," Blemish said. "What can I do for you, Mr. Adams?"

"I'm looking for a man named Dave Britton."

"And you have some reason to believe that he's here?" the little man asked.

"Possibly."

"Well," Blemish said, "he's not."

"Do you know him?"

"I know the name," Blemish said.

"So he lives in town?"

"Outside of town."

That was one similarity between William Reardon and Britton.

"Is he a rancher?"

"Hardly," Blemish said. "I believe you'd get more information from the sheriff—or a bartender. That is all I know."

It was either all the undertaker knew, or all he wanted to say.

"I see. Well, thanks anyway."

"Will you be in town long?"

"I don't think so," Clint said. "It depends on what I find."

"Shall I keep some pine boxes ready?" Blemish asked.

Clint left without answering the man's question.

EIGHT

So Clint had his choice, the local law or a bartender. If he went to a bartender for the information, and later found Britton dead, he'd have a lot of explaining to do to the local sheriff. So he was better off going to the law.

He rode to the sheriff's office, which he had passed on the way into town. He draped Eclipse's reins over a hitching post so nobody could get any ideas and entered the office.

It was empty.

He walked around, checked the cell block, looked at the sheriff's desk. At least there was no dust covering everything, so he knew the office was in use. Also there was still some heat on the coffeepot, which was empty. Or almost empty. When he opened it, he smelled burning coffee. He moved the pot off the stove.

He went back outside, looked up and down the street, wondering if the lawman was making rounds, or was in one of the saloons.

He decided to check the saloon. He unlooped Eclipse's

reins and walked the horse down the block to the first of the two saloons he had seen when he rode into town.

Outside he once again looped Eclipse's reins around a post and went inside. He went to the bar and suddenly wanted a beer very badly. He'd been running ever since he received that telegram over two weeks before, and there was going to be a lot more running in the future. Why the killer chose him, he didn't know. He wondered if and when he found the man, would he know him? Probably. Why would a stranger want to run him around this way?

"Beer," he told the bartender.

"Comin' up."

The bar had a few patrons, none of whom paid any attention to him, which suited him.

"There ya go," the bartender said, putting a beer in front of him.

"I'm looking for the sheriff," he said to the man. "Have you seen him today?"

"Earlier," the bartender said. "Not lately. Do you know him?"

"Never met him," Clint said. "I don't even know his name."

"Sheppard," the bartender said, "Sheriff Joe Sheppard."

"Has he been the sheriff here for very long?" Clint asked.

"A couple of years," the bartender said. "He's kind of a young guy."

"How young?"

"Um, I'm thirty-five—he's a few years younger than me."

"Okay," Clint said, "any idea where I might find him?"

"He could be doing his rounds."

"Where does he go when he has time off?"

"No time off that I know of," the bartender said.

"Does he have a deputy?"

"We're a small town," the man said, "there's no money in the budget for a deputy. It's just him."

"Okay," Clint said, "what's your name?"

"Nolan."

"Mr. Nolan—"

"Just Nolan."

"Okay, Nolan," Clint said, "maybe you can help me."

"Before I do," Nolan said, "who are you?"

Clint hesitated, then said, "My name is Clint Adams."

"The Gunsmith?"

"That's right."

"What the hell are you doin' in this town?" Nolan asked.

"Maybe if you let me ask my questions, you'll find out," Clint said.

"Okay, yeah, go ahead," Nolan said. "You want another beer first?"

"Yes, I do," Clint said.

Nolan drew another beer and set it in front of Clint.

"Okay," he said, "shoot."

"Do you know a man named Dave Britton?"

"Sure, Dave, he comes in here . . . a lot."

"How often is a lot?"

"Like, every day."

"Has he been in today?"

"Now that you mention it, no. He shoulda been."

"Why does he come in every day if he lives outside of town?" Clint asked.

"Because that's what drunks do," Nolan said. "They drink every day."

"He's the town drunk?"

"We might be a small town," Nolan said, "but we're not that small. We have town drunks. He's one of them."

NINE

"Nolan, if I can't find the sheriff, who could take me out to Dave Britton's house?"

"I can getcha somebody," Nolan said. "If you come back later and let me know—"

"Okay," Clint said. "I'll take a look around town and see if I can locate the sheriff. If not, I'll come back."

"I'll have somebody ready to go," Nolan said.

"I'll pay him."

"No problem, Mr. Adams."

Clint finished his second beer and paid for both, even though Nolan tried to let him have them on the house.

"Are you sure he's the Gunsmith?" Randy Wilkins asked.

"Well," Nolan said, "he said he was. Why would anybody claim to be the Gunsmith if he wasn't?"

"For the fame?"

"Not me," Nolan said. "Claiming to be Adams would paint a target on any man's back. Naw, he was tellin' the truth."

"Well, I'll be damned," Wilkins said. "The Gunsmith. And I'm gonna get to meet him?"

"You're gonna get to take him out to Dave Britton's place."

"What for?"

"You'll find out when you get there."

"What about the sheriff?"

"Don't know where he is."

"I could find 'im—"

"Then you won't be able to take Adams out there," Nolan said. "Why don't you just wait like I said, and we'll all find out what's goin' on."

Clint walked around town, checked the other, smaller saloon, but found no sign of Sheriff Joe Sheppard. He checked the office again, but when he found it empty, he finally gave up and went back to the saloon.

There was a man standing at the bar with Nolan when he walked in. He was about thirty, dressed in trail clothes, wearing a well-worn gun that he was too young to have worn out himself.

"This my guide?" he asked.

"This is him," Nolan said. "Randy Wilkins, meet Clint Adams."

"Sure is a pleasure to meet ya, Mr. Adams."

"You know the way to Dave Britton's place?"

"Sure do."

"Let's go, then."

"Now?"

"The sooner the better. Where's your horse?"

"Well . . . outside—"

"Like I said," Clint cut him off, "let's go."

* * *

They rode about a mile outside of town. Clint figured he could have made the trip with directions. For some reason, the bartender wanted this fella to go with him.

"This it?" Clint asked.

"Ain't much of a house, is it?" Wilkins said.

It was a shack.

"Stay here," Clint said, dismounting.

"I can't come in?"

"I have a feeling I know what I'm going to find inside," Clint said. "Take my advice and stay here."

"Yessir."

"Good," Clint said. "Hold my horse's reins and don't talk to him."

"Why not?"

"He doesn't like strangers."

He walked to the front door, found it ajar, but knocked anyway. He didn't knock a second time. He pushed open the door and went inside. There were only two rooms in the shack, and not much in the way of furniture. The body was in the center of the floor. Shot in the back.

He realized he should have let Wilkins come in. He had no way of knowing if this was Britton or not.

He went to the door and stuck his head out.

"Randy? You want to come in here?"

"Why?"

"I just need you to look at something."

Wilkins dismounted, tied off the horses, and approached the shack.

"What am I lookin' at?" he asked.

"A body," Clint said.

"What for?"

"I need to know if it's Dave Britton."

"He's dead?"

"You tell me."

Wilkins entered the house. Clint went to the body and turned it over enough for Wilkin to see the face.

"That's him," he said. "That's Dave Britton."

Clint let the body flop back over onto its belly.

"Okay, Randy, wait outside."

"We got to find the sheriff."

"I spent the morning trying to find the sheriff," Clint said. "You got any idea where he is?"

"No, sir."

"Then wait outside. I just need to look around a bit, and then we'll go and look for him."

Wilkins went out.

Clint went through the dead man's pockets, then searched the shack. He found nothing helpful. On top of that he found no paper or pencils, and no reading material. He had the feeling that Dave Britton hadn't known how to read or write.

On the other hand, William Reardon had been a rancher who did a lot of paperwork. What could these two men have had in common to make the same killer shoot them both? And why in the back?

Clint left the shack, found Wilkins standing with the horses.

"All right," he said, "let's find that badge toter."

TEN

They got back to town and stopped at the saloon to see Nolan.

"What happened?" the bartender asked. "Did you see Britton?"

"We saw him," Clint said.

"Dave's dead, Nolan."

"Dead?" Nolan looked at Clint.

"I didn't shoot him," Clint said. "I found him that way. Have you seen the sheriff yet?"

"Yeah, I did. He was in here for a drink a little while ago."

"And do you know where he is now?"

"Well, he said he was goin' back to his office."

"And did you tell him about me?"

"I—well, um, yeah, I did, but—"

"That's okay," Clint said. "Don't worry about it. I'll just go and see if I find him in his office."

Clint took a few dollars out of his pocket and gave it to Wilkins.

"Thanks, Randy."

"Huh? Oh, sure, Mr. Adams." Wilkins took the money. "Thanks a lot."

Clint started for the door.

"You want me to come with ya?" Wilkins asked.

"No," Clint said, "I know where the sheriff's office is."

"Yeah, but I thought, ya know, maybe you'd want me to tell him what we found."

Clint turned to face Wilkins, then said, "Well, yeah, that'd be good, Randy." He put his hand in his pocket again.

"That's okay, Mr. Adams," Wilkins said. "You ain't gotta pay me again."

"Thanks, Randy."

A man Clint took to be Sheriff Sheppard looked up from his desk as Clint and Randy Wilkins walked into the office.

"Randy," he said, "what brings you here?"

"Mr. Adams and me got something to tell you, Sheriff," Randy said.

"Adams?"

"Clint Adams," Clint said.

Sheppard sat back with a startled look, then frowned and leaned forward.

"The Gunsmith?"

"That's right," Wilkins said.

"Well . . . what brings you to town, Mr. Adams?" the lawman asked.

"I was looking for a man named Dave Britton," Clint answered.

"Britton? Why would you be lookin' for a drunk like him—you ain't lookin' ta kill him, are ya?"

"He's already dead, Sheriff," Wilkins said. "We done found him that way."

"Randy . . ." Clint said.

Wilkins shut up and looked at Clint, wondering if he'd said something wrong.

"I think I'd like to talk to the sheriff alone," Clint finally finished.

"Oh, uh, sure, Mr. Adams," Randy said. "Sure thing. I'll just see ya later at the saloon, huh?"

"Sure," Clint said, "maybe."

He waited for Wilkins to leave, then turned to the lawman and said, "I should show you a few things first . . ."

ELEVEN

Clint showed the lawman the telegram, the letter, and the list, and gave him time to look at them all.

"This is crazy," the man said, handing them all back.

"I know it."

"Why would Britton even be on a list like that?" Sheppard asked. "He was a nothing, a nobody, a . . . drunk."

"I was hoping you'd tell me that," Clint replied.

"Me? I ain't got no idea. Sorry."

"Then I guess I'll just have to move on to the next location."

"Where's that?"

"Tennessee," Clint said. "A town called Brethren."

"Never heard of it."

"Me neither."

"What's the next man's name?"

Clint took the list out and unfolded it.

"Beckett, Andrew Beckett."

"Never heard of him either."

"Likewise."

"Stayin' in town tonight?" Sheppard asked.

"Yes, me and my horse need to have some rest."

"I'll go out and collect poor Dave's body and take him over to Blemish. Have you met Blemish?"

"Briefly."

"He's a funny little man, but a good undertaker. Did you take a look around out there?"

"Just enough to see if there was anything helpful there."

"Well, I guess I don't need to worry about who killed him. Not since you got that note."

"I'll be leaving in the morning," Clint said, "so I'll be at the hotel if you need me. Uh, how many hotels do you have?"

"Two," the sheriff said, "one's as good—or bad—as the other."

"Well, I'll be in one of them, if you need me," Clint said, "but I'll be leaving at first light."

"Think you're gonna beat your killer there?"

"I doubt it," Clint said. "He's always got a head start on me."

"Why don't you jump ahead of him?"

"I may have to do something like that," Clint said, "but if I do and he finds out, I'm taking a chance that he'll mix up the order."

"And then what?"

"Well, he's supposed to be killing them in order," Clint said. "At least, that's what he claims. If he decides to start mixing up the order, I'll probably never catch him."

"I don't envy you, havin' to chase him all over the

country," Sheppard said. "And who knows how long you'll be doin' it?"

He had a good point.

Clint took Eclipse to the livery, and got himself a room at one of the hotels. After that he went back to the saloon for a beer. He also hoped that Nolan or Wilkins would be able to steer him toward a good steak.

"Hey, Mr. Adams," the bartender called out as he entered.

It was later in the day, so the place was much more crowded than it had been before. Nolan beckoned Clint to the bar.

"Beer on the house?" he asked, setting it on the bar.

"Don't mind if I do."

Clint picked it up, turned, and looked around.

"Where's Randy?" he asked.

"I ain't seen him since he left here with you," Nolan said.

Clint noticed there were two girls working the floor, a blonde and a redhead. The blonde seemed to notice him at the same time and came over.

"Is this him?" she asked Nolan.

"This is him," the bartender said. "Louisa, meet the Gunsmith."

"Mr. Gunsmith," she said, sticking out her hand.

"My name is Clint."

"Clint," she said as they shook hands. "I'd buy you a drink, but you seem to have one."

"Well, then," he said, "let me buy you one."

"Nolan," she said, "I'll have a beer."

He knew she had come over to him on her own. If she was working him for the saloon, she would have ordered champagne.

"Comin' up."

She pressed up close to Clint, hip to hip, while she waited for her beer.

"How long are you gonna be in our little town, Clint?" she asked him.

"Only 'til morning," he said. "I'll be riding out at first light."

"You must be goin' someplace important to be in such a hurry to leave."

"I'm heading for Tennessee," he said. "I'll find out how important it is when I get there."

Nolan brought her a beer. She picked it up and held it out in a toast.

"Here's hopin' you enjoy the time you have left in town," she said.

He clinked glasses with her and said, "Maybe you can help me out with that."

She sipped her beer and said, "Maybe I can."

TWELVE

Louisa accompanied Clint back to his hotel later that night. Clint kept a sharp eye out for anyone following, or waiting for them near the hotel. Of course, she could have been going back to his hotel willingly, but there was also the possibility that she had some partners following or lying in wait.

By the time they reached the hotel, though, he hadn't noticed anyone. Nevertheless, when they entered his room, he made sure the door was locked, and then hung his gun on the bedpost, where it would be within easy reach.

"You think you're gonna need that?" she asked.

"You never know," he said.

"Well," she said, approaching him and putting her arms around him, "you won't need it to get me into bed."

"Maybe," he said, encircling her waist, "I'll need it to get you out."

She laughed, pulled his head down to kiss him.

She was not tall, about five-five, and fit in his arms

nicely. In holding her, he found that she was more solid than she appeared. He started to undo the stays on her dress, wanting to get a look at her naked. She did what she could to help him without breaking the kiss.

Finally, her dress dropped to the floor and his hands were on her pale skin. She had round, solid breasts, not overly large but nice and heavy in his hands. He broke the kiss to look at her pink nipples, bent down to lick first one then the other. A shiver ran through her as she started undoing his shirt, and then his belt. They worked together to divest him of all his clothes, and then pressed their naked bodies together in a hot embrace.

She reached between them to grasp his cock in her hand and seemed to like what she found.

"Oh, my!" she said. She kissed his chest, his belly, then went to her knees to fondle his penis in both hands while she kissed and licked it. It swelled in her hands, and then in her mouth as she sucked it in.

"Mmmm," she said as her head bobbed back and forth, sliding his cock wetly in and out of her mouth.

He groaned as she continued to suckle him, and slid one hand down to cup his testicles. He began to move his hips in unison with the sucking motion of her mouth and head. She slid her hands behind him to cup his ass cheeks as the avid sucking began to produce loud, wet sounds.

He looked down at her blond head as she bobbed up and down on him, and when he couldn't take it anymore, he bent, slid his hands beneath her arms, and lifted her to her feet. Once there, he kept going, lifted her off her feet, turned, and deposited her on the bed.

"Oooh," she said as she bounced.

He got on the bed with her, spread her legs, picked one up, and put it over her shoulder, then leaned into her fragrant crotch and pressed his face to her. Her pubic hair was extremely blond, and glistened a bit with her wetness. He probed her with his tongue, then licked her up and down until she was writhing beneath him, wetting the sheet thoroughly. He let her leg drop, but stayed where he was between them, keeping them wide so he could get to his knees between them and thrust his hard cock into her.

"Oh, Jesus!" she shrieked as he pierced her.

She closed her hands into fists, gathering up the sheet and hanging on while he pounded in and out of her.

"Oooh, God," she moaned. He reached beneath her to cup her ass in an attempt to drive himself into her even deeper. She moaned and gasped as she tried to breathe, but he was literally fucking the air out of her lungs.

"Jesus," she said at one point, placing her hands against his chest and trying to push him off, "you're not lettin' me breathe."

"Breathing's overrated," he rasped to her. His mouth and throat were also raw as he was having trouble taking breaths himself. He realized he was going to have to ease up a bit or they'd both pass out.

He slowed his pace down, began to take her in long, slow strokes so that they were both able to catch their breath a bit.

"Mmm, that's it," she said, "that's nice."

"You get a man all worked up, you know," he said.

"And you do the same thing to a girl," she said, "but we have to make sure we can finish what we start."

"Oh, don't worry," he promised, "we'll finish what we started . . . and then start all over again."

"Ooh," she said, closing her legs around him, "my hero . . ."

They finished and started, finished and started a few times before they finally took a rest, lying side by side. He was glad no one had kicked in the door to try and kill him. He would have been very disappointed if that had happened.

"Oh my," she said, "by the time you ride out of town in the morning, I won't be able to walk straight."

"Riding might be a little bit of a problem for me, too," he said.

"Oh, good," she said. "Then you'll have to stay to recover."

"I wish I could," he said, "but I really have to get going."

"Why?" she asked. "Is it a life-and-death thing?"

"Actually," he replied, "it is. More than you know."

THIRTEEN

Perry Silver rode into Brethren, Tennessee, on a big midnight black horse, which took all the attention off him. All anyone remembered later was the horse, which was his plan.

Brethren was a thriving town, growing by leaps and bounds over the last few years. Just riding down the main street, you could smell the newly cut lumber that had been used to erect some of the newer buildings.

Silver didn't know if the town was religious, as the name might imply. What he had to do, however, had nothing to do with religion, so it didn't matter to him one way or another.

Brethren was bigger than the other towns had been, so it was likely that this would take a bit longer. It might even make it necessary for him to stay in town overnight, at least. He hoped to avoid hotels, but a town this size would probably have some rooming houses available to strangers.

Silver stopped in front of the first saloon he came to,

a big place called The White Stetson Saloon. He tied off his horse and entered the saloon. There was enough activity going on that he didn't draw very much attention. He was not a big man, or a physically demonstrative man, who drew attention simply by entering a room. This worked in his favor.

He went to the bar and ordered a beer. When the bartender brought it, he asked him about rooming houses.

"Sure," the barman said, "there are a couple. Mrs. Costner's got one at the far end of town, and then Libby Callahan made her home into one after her husband died. The rest of the houses around here are all single families."

Libby's sounded like the one he wanted.

"Can you give me directions to both?" he asked.

"Sure thing."

The bartender reeled off the directions and Silver memorized them. He finished his beer, thanked the bartender, and left to check out the rooming houses.

He stopped at Libby Callahan's first, dismounted, and knocked on the front door. There was nothing out front that indicated it was a rooming house, but he was sure he had followed the directions properly.

A handsome woman in her forties answered the door and smiled at him.

"Can I help you?"

"I was told in town that this is a rooming house?" he asked.

"That's correct."

"Do you have a room available?"

"I have a couple," she said. "Are you alone?"

"Oh, yeah," he said. "I'm alone."

She looked past him.

"Your horse?"

He nodded.

"You'll have to put him up in one of the livery stables in town. I can direct you to the closest one."

"Okay."

"Come on in," she said.

"Let me get my saddlebags."

He got his saddlebags off the horse, then followed the woman into the house and to his room.

"Very nice," he said, looking around. A bed, a dresser, a table, and one chair. And clean.

"Better than any hotel," she said.

"I believe it."

"How long will you be staying?"

"Just one night, hopefully."

"Passing through?"

"That's right. I have . . . business elsewhere."

"Well, breakfast is at eight, and supper's at five. You'll have to get lunch—but you won't be here for lunch, will you?"

"No, just supper tonight and breakfast in the morning."

They discussed money and he paid her in advance for one night. After that she gave him directions to the nearest livery stable.

She walked him to the front door and said, "You won't need a key. The door's unlocked until ten. After that you can't get in."

"At all?"

"At all," she said. "And no girls in the room."

"That's fine," he said. "I'm not here looking for a girl."

"No? Who are you here looking for?"

He stared at her for a moment, then asked, "Do you know a man named Andrew Beckett?"

FOURTEEN

Clint rode into Brethren, Tennessee, and was impressed with what he saw. Unlike the other two towns he'd been to, it might take him a little longer to find the man he was looking for.

He'd given the matter a lot of thought during the days and nights it had taken him to get from Kansas to Tennessee. If this was simply a replay of the last two towns, with him simply finding the men dead, he was going to have to make a change. Just riding from town to town to find dead men would not cut it. He had to try to do something to save these men, and something to find the killer.

After Beckett, there were seven more men on the death list. One thing he was considering was calling on seven of his friends, having each of them go to find one of the seven men and not only warning them, but keeping them safe until Clint could get there. Maybe talking to them and comparing notes would give him some insight into who the killer might be.

Clint rode to a livery stable at the end of the main

street and left Eclipse in the care of a capable-looking hostler. From there he took his saddlebags and rifle and registered at the Haystacks Hotel, across the street from The White Stetson Saloon.

From his room he looked down at the traffic in the main street in front of the hotel. Like the first time, he'd stop at the sheriff's office first. In Kansas, he'd stopped at the undertaker's first. Both times all he'd succeeded in doing was finding a body.

If Andrew Beckett was already dead, it wouldn't make a difference if he stopped at the sheriff's first, the under-taker's, or a saloon. Dead was dead.

Feeling frustrated, he left the hotel and crossed over to The White Stetson. It was afternoon, still a couple of hours from the time the saloons would be jumping, but this one was close. It was a big place, more than half full, and noisy. A piano was being played in a corner, gaming tables were coming alive, four or five girls were working the floor, and there were two bartenders behind the bar.

Clint found himself a space at the bar and waved for one of the bartenders to come over. One was young, in his twenties, the other in his fifties. The young one came over to him.

"Whataya have?"

"Beer."

"Comin' up."

He came right back with the beer, moving quickly but not spilling a drop.

"Anythin' else?"

"Yeah," Clint said, "do you know a man named Beck-ett?"

"Beckett?"

"Yes, Andrew Beckett."

"Um, lemme ask Barney. He knows everybody."

"Okay, thanks."

The boy went over to the older bartender, who Clint assumed was Barney. Clint took his beer in hand and turned to survey the room. Covers were still coming off the gaming tables, and dealers were setting up their games. He looked back to the bartenders, but they were both gone. Then, while he was watching, the one named Barney reappeared again, but the young one was still gone.

Clint waved at the older bartender, but he didn't seem to see him. He waved again, then called out, "Barney."

The man looked at him, seemed to be nervous about something. Clint waved him over.

"Yessir?"

"Are you Barney?"

"Yessir."

"I asked the other bartender about Andrew Beckett. He said you'd know who he is."

"Beckett?"

"That's right," Clint said. "Come on, man, do you know him or not?"

"Um, I think so," Barney said. "Yeah, he—he lives in town."

"Right in town?" Clint asked.

"Well, no," Barney said, "I mean, hereabouts."

"Well, where?"

"Um—oh, hey, I gotta go to work. I'll—I'll be right back."

He hurried down the bar to serve somebody else.

Something was wrong, Clint thought. The man was

too nervous for no reason, and the young bartender had not come back yet.

He was about to call out to him again when he heard a voice from behind him.

"Just stand fast, mister," he was told. "No sudden moves."

Clint froze.

"Put your hands up."

He did so.

"What's going on?" he asked.

"That's what I want to know," the voice said. "I'm Sheriff Busey."

"There's no need for this, Sheriff," Clint said. "I only just got to town—"

"And already you're asking about Andrew Beckett."

"Is there a law against that?"

"There is when Andrew Beckett is dead," the sheriff said.

FIFTEEN

"Turn around."

Clint did so, saw a fiftyish man with gray hair under a gray hat, pointing a gun at him. He noticed that the gun was very steady.

"Who are you?" the sheriff asked.

"My name is Clint Adams."

The saloon had become quiet when the sheriff arrived, so everyone in the place heard that.

"Adams?" the sheriff asked.

"That's right."

"The Gunsmith?"

"Yeah."

The sheriff hesitated, then said, "You're lyin'."

"Nope, I'm not."

"Put your hands up, away from your gun."

Clint obeyed, even though he really only needed to raise one hand to keep it away from his gun.

"Take his gun."

The sheriff had a deputy with him who stepped forward, nervously plucked Clint's gun from his holster.

"Okay," Busey said, "let's take a walk over to my office and we'll find out who you really are."

"How are we going to do that?" Clint asked.

"I don't know," the sheriff said. "Let's just get over to my office first."

"Okay, Sheriff," Clint said, "I'm not going to give you any trouble."

"That's good to know," Busey said. "Let's go."

The deputy led the way.

When they got to the office, Clint expected to be put into a cell. Instead, the sheriff just told him to have a seat. Then he sat behind his desk and put Clint's gun in a drawer.

"Okay," he said, "so you're Clint Adams."

"You mean, you believed me?"

"Well, yeah," Busey said. "Who'd lie about a thing like that? It's like painting a bull's-eye on your back."

"So, why did you—"

"You didn't want the whole saloon knowin' you were the Gunsmith, did you? That's a sure way of havin' somebody come after you."

"You might be right about that. Can I have my gun back?"

"Not right now. I came over to the saloon because Willie—that's the other bartender—came running over here and told me somebody was in the saloon asking about Andrew Beckett."

"And Andrew Beckett is dead."

The sheriff stared at him for a moment, then asked, "What do you know about that?"

Clint took the telegram, letter, and list from his pocket and handed them over. He had put a line through the first two names.

The sheriff read everything, then looked at the list again.

"I assume the first two names on this list are dead?" he asked.

"That's right."

"Shot in the back?"

"Right again."

Busey put all the papers on the desk, then opened his drawer, took out Clint's gun, and laid it on top.

"Giving me back my gun?"

"Nobody would fake this story, and those," the sheriff said, pointing to the papers.

Clint took his gun and holstered it, folded the papers, and put them back in his pocket.

"Can you tell me what happened to Beckett? Who he was?" Clint asked.

"He was a rancher hereabouts, got a place about five miles east of town."

"Rich?"

"No."

"But not poor. Not a drunk?"

"No! He was a respected businessman here in town," Busey said. "Why, were those others—"

"The second one," Clint said. "He was a drunk in Dexter, Kansas. The first man was a rancher, like Beckett."

"Dexter, Kansas," Busey said with a frown. "That don't mean nothin' to me."

"Didn't to me either," Clint said. "The only thing I

see that these men had in common is that they all lived outside of town."

"That ain't no reason to kill 'em all," Busey said. "What about these other seven? You gonna warn them?"

Clint hesitated long enough for Busey to say, "You gotta warn 'em."

Clint told Sheriff Busey what the letter writer had said about that.

"Well, how's he gonna know if you send a telegram?" the lawman asked.

"I don't know," Clint said. "I don't know if he's a one-man show, or if he's got people working with him."

"I don't see where you got much of a choice, Adams," Busey said. "You got three dead men on your hands right now. How many more you want?"

"You know," Clint said defensively, "I could've just ignored the whole thing. Let each of you local lawmen deal with it."

"That's true," Busey said, "but the time for that has passed, don't you think?"

"That's the problem," Clint said. "I do think that. I'm stuck in this for the long haul, but I've got to act carefully."

"Well . . . I don't know what to tell you," Busey said. "I guess you gotta make your own decisions. You wanna see the body?"

"Yeah," Clint said. "Where is it?"

"The undertaker's." The lawman stood up. "Come on, I'll take you over there."

They stood up and left the office together.

SIXTEEN

Clint looked down at the body of Andrew Beckett, then turned and walked back into the main room of the undertaker's office. This undertaker—unlike Mr. Blemish from Dexter, Kansas—looked like an undertaker—tall and cadaverously thin. Clint wondered if men who did this job just developed that way over the years.

"When is he supposed to be buried?" he asked the sheriff.

"Today, actually."

"So when was he killed?"

"Two days ago."

"Two days?"

"Is that the closest you've been to him?"

"I'm not sure," Clint said. "I mean, I don't know how long the other men were dead before I got there. I may be two days behind him all along."

"You should be able to make up some of that time," Busey said.

Yeah, Clint thought, if I mount up on Eclipse right now

and ride like hell to the next town. He was unwilling to ride the big Darley Arabian to death, not even to save a life. That spoke volumes about how much store he put in that horse. He wasn't sure other people would understand.

"I've got a lot of thinking to do," Clint said.

"I just hope somebody else doesn't die while you're thinkin'," Busey said.

Clint had supper alone that night, studied the list while he ate a passable bowl of beef stew in the hotel dining room.

For the next stop he had to travel all the way back west to Denver, then northwest to Minnesota, then south to Saint Louis . . . it probably was time to press the railroad into use. But he didn't want to leave Eclipse in Brethren. He would prefer to leave the horse in Denver, where he'd know he was being well cared for.

By the time he finished his supper, he'd decided to take a chance with sending a telegram. He'd compose one in his room and send it the next morning to his friend, Talbot Roper, in Denver. Roper was a private investigator. Maybe they could save the life of the man in Denver. His name was Daniel Dolan, another name Clint had never heard. But maybe Roper would know something.

Even if the killer caught him sending a telegram to Roper and started mixing up his order of kills, he might still be able to save the life of some of the men on the list.

And the one woman.

In his room he studied the list again. There was only one woman on it, and she was last. Her name was Amanda Tolliver, and she lived in San Francisco. If he continued to follow the order of the list, that would be his last stop. And no doubt, if he continued to follow the list, he'd arrive there to find her already dead.

That was unacceptable.

It was time for him to take a chance, and make a change in his approach. When he arrived in Denver, he could also press Roper into service, pick the man's superior brain to see what he had to offer in the way of a solution to the problem.

Maybe it was time to stop chasing the victims, and start chasing the killer.

SEVENTEEN

Talbot Roper opened the door to his Denver office and entered. Seated at the reception desk was a girl he'd never seen before.

"Mr. Roper?" she asked.

"That's right."

She smiled brightly and stood up—all five foot two and twenty years of her.

"I'm here for the receptionist job."

"How did you get in?"

"The door was open."

"What?"

"It was open. I knocked and it opened, so I thought I'd come in and sit down and wait for you."

"There's no way that door should have been open," Roper said. "Where's Justine?"

"Who?"

"The woman who was working here."

"As far as I know," she said, "you need a receptionist."

Justine had been working there three months. The night before, when they had their latest fight, he didn't believe that it would be their last, as she had said. But if she left the door open behind her when she left, it looked like this time it was for real.

"How did you find out so soon I needed a new girl?" he asked.

"Um, my mother is friends with Mrs. Batchelder and she heard you were looking for someone."

That explained it. Mrs. Batchelder had an employment agency down the street, and she had sent him Justine three months ago. Justine must have told her that she was leaving.

"Okay," he said, "what's your name?"

"Wendy."

"Did Mrs. Batchelder tell you what the job is?" he asked.

"Yes. Screening people who come in to see you, taking messages, some filing . . . basically doing anything you need me to do."

"And what did she tell you about me personally?"

"Oh," Wendy said, looking down. "She said you were a good man, very handsome, but hard to get along with."

"We'll see about that," he said. "I'm going into my office. I'll have some work for you in a little while."

"Those files on your desk?"

He'd started into his office, stopped in the doorway. He had left a stack of files on his desk that Justine had not put away. They were gone.

"What about them?" he asked.

"I assumed you wanted them filed, so I put them away."

"You did."

She nodded and said, "Was that all right?"

"Sure," he said, "that's perfect."

He walked into his office and sat behind his desk. She came in behind him.

"Was there something else?" he asked.

"Yessir," she said. "This came for you about half an hour ago."

He reached out and took what she was offering him. It was a telegram.

"Did you read this?"

"Just enough to make sure it was for you."

"Okay, Wendy," he said. "Thank you."

"Yessir."

She turned and went out, closing his office door behind her. He wondered how long it would be before he drove her away?

He turned his attention to the telegram. It was from Clint Adams, his closest friend.

WILL BE IN TOWN THIS THURS **STOP** PLEASE
CHECK ON A MAN NAMED DANIEL DOLAN FOR ME
STOP WILL NEED INFORMATION AS SOON AS I
ARRIVE **STOP**

It was Thursday. The telegram didn't say what time Clint would arrive, or where he was coming from, but Roper knew one thing. When he did arrive, he'd be staying at the Denver House Hotel. It was where he always stayed when he was in town.

Roper looked at the man's name again—Daniel Dolan. It didn't mean anything to him, but if Clint needed information on the man, that's what Roper would get for his friend.

He stood up, straightened his jacket, and went out to reception. Wendy was sitting behind her desk with her hands in her lap. She brightened when she saw him.

"Wendy, I have to go out," he said. "If Mr. Adams gets here before I get back, keep him here. Make him comfortable."

"Yessir."

He started for the door, then came back.

"If you go out for lunch, leave a note."

"For you, or for Mr. Adams?" she asked.

"Both."

"Yessir."

He was about to tell her to stop saying "Yessir," to him, but he decided he liked it.

"If I go for lunch, I will bring it back here and eat it," she said. "Don't worry. I will be here to greet Mr. Adams."

"Okay," Roper said, "just remember that he's my friend. Treat him with respect."

"Yessir. What's his full name?"

"Clint Adams."

He waited to see if she knew the name, but there was no recognition whatsoever on her face.

She was young.

Very young.

After Roper left, Wendy went into his office and began going through his desk drawers. She had been told he was handsome, and that was true, but she had a job to do, and she intended to do it.

Maybe later there would be time for some fun.

Much later.

EIGHTEEN

Clint arrived in Denver, arranged for Eclipse to be taken from the train to the stables of the Denver House Hotel. He did not want to ride Eclipse through the streets of Denver. A lot of them were cobblestoned, and too well traveled. The streets were not necessarily well cared for, and there were too many things that could go wrong.

Once he'd made his arrangements, he took a cab to the Denver House. He checked in with a desk clerk he didn't know and went to his two-room suite. The Denver House was one of the finest hotels in Denver, and—except for San Francisco and New York—the only time he splurged on a good hotel.

He washed up, changed his shirt, and took his Colt New Line out of his saddlebags. When he was in Denver, he didn't wear his holster. He preferred to wear his little hideaway .25 caliber.

He tucked the little gun into his belt at the small of

his back, put on his jacket, and left the room. Roper's office was a short cab ride, or a long walk. He decided to grab a cab in front of the hotel. He hoped that the private detective would be able to help him with his problem.

When he got to Roper's office, he knocked on the door and entered. There was a young girl seated behind the desk when he walked in. He didn't know her. Roper went through several girls a year. It was hard to understand, because Roper loved women and they loved him—but he couldn't get along with the ones who worked for him.

"Hello," he said.

"Hi," she said brightly.

"Is Roper in?"

"He had to go out, but he'll be back anytime now. Are you Mr. Adams?"

"That's right."

She stood up quickly.

"I've been instructed to make you comfortable," she said. "Can I get you anything?"

"No, I'm fine," he said. "I just need to talk to Roper."

"Well, he went out earlier today. I expect him back shortly."

"There's a small saloon across the street," Clint said. "I'll wait there."

"Oh, but I can get you anything you—"

"No, that's fine," he said. "What's your name?"

"Wendy."

"I'll be fine in the saloon, Wendy. I'm just going to

nurse a beer until he gets back. Will you tell him I'm there?"

"Yessir, I'll tell him that, but—"

"Thank you."

He turned and left, and Wendy couldn't think of anything to say to make him stay.

The saloon across the street was new. It hadn't been there the last time he was at Roper's office. When he walked in, he saw that it was small and clean, with a few businessmen drinking at the bar, one or two seated at tables.

He went to the bar and the businessmen nodded at him. He nodded back. Not exactly the greeting you got in most Western saloons.

"What can I get you, sir?" the bartender asked. He was wearing a white shirt and a tie, and his hair was parted in the middle.

"Beer," Clint said.

"Right away."

The bartender quickly brought Clint a beer. He thanked the man and then carried it to a table. Instead of his usual back table away from the windows, he chose one next to a stained glass window. He could see out through one of the panes, but no one could see in. He'd be able to see when Roper arrived.

He had the papers in his pocket—the telegram, the letter, the list. He also had the note he'd received at the hotel after the first killing. Oddly, there had been no notes left after the second and third killings. What was the point of that first note, then?

He knew he was taking a big chance bringing Roper

in, but he didn't feel he had any choice. And he knew he'd have to bring in some others, but from this point on—if he agreed—all future telegrams would come from Roper.

Clint nursed the beer until it was warm and there was only half left. The bartender came over and asked, "Is the beer all right, sir? Can I get you a cold one?"

"Yeah," Clint said, "that'd be good. I'm just waiting for someone."

"I understand, sir." He picked up the warm beer. "I'll bring a cold beer for you while you wait for your lady friend."

"I'm not waiting for a woman. What made you think that?" Clint asked.

"I'm sorry, sir," the bartender said. "It's just that a lot of gentlemen meet ladies here."

"Ladies?"

"Yes, sir," the man said. "I'll be right back with your beer."

Clint looked around. He still saw several men seated at tables, waiting. At the bar the two men he took to be businessmen were still there, not speaking to each other. Apparently, all these men were waiting.

"Here you go, sir," the bartender said, putting a fresh beer down in front of him.

"Thanks."

"I meant no offense, sir."

"None taken."

"Thank you, sir."

The bartender went to check on his other customers.

Clint looked out the clear pane and saw Roper entering his office. Moments later the private investigator came out again and started across the street toward the saloon.

Clint heard the shot and saw Roper go down. In a flash, he was out of his chair.

NINETEEN

Clint's feet hit the cobblestones and he had his gun out. Now he wished he had the Colt, and not his little .25.

"Roper" he yelled. "Tal! Are you hit?"

Roper looked up, saw Clint coming toward him. He held out his hand.

"I'm okay, I'm not hit!" he shouted.

Clint reached his friend and crouched down by him, hoping to shield him from any more bullets.

"Did you see where the shot came from?" Clint asked.

"No," Roper said. "Clint, for Chrissake, get off the street!"

"Come on," Clint said, "back to your office."

"No," Roper said, "the saloon. Come on."

Clint pulled Roper to his feet and they both ran to the saloon.

"Hey, wait!" the bartender shouted. "No shooting in here!"

"Nobody's going to shoot," Clint said, putting his gun away.

Clint looked around. The place was empty. All the "businessmen" were gone.

Clint and Roper went to a back table this time, and Clint told the bartender, "Two whiskeys."

"Comin' up."

Clint looked at Roper across the table.

"You okay?"

Roper looked down at his knee.

"Scraped my knee, tore my pants, but that's about it," the detective said.

"Where'd the shot come from?"

"I don't know," Roper said. "It didn't hit the ground, so it didn't come from above."

"Are you working on something now?" Clint asked hopefully.

"No, not really," Roper said. "I'm between cases, which is why I went out as soon as I got your telegram."

"As soon as you got it?"

"Yes," Roper said. "This morning."

Clint sat back in his chair to allow the bartender to set down the whiskeys.

"Two beers, also," he told the man.

"Right away."

"Tal," Clint said, "I sent that telegram three days ago."

"I swear, Clint, I only got it today."

Clint sipped his whiskey.

"What's going on?" Roper asked. "Why did you need me to check on Daniel Dolan?"

"Dolan," Clint said. "What did you find out?"

"Only that he was a businessman here in Denver," Roper said.

"Rich or poor?"

"Well off," Roper said. "Not what you'd call rich, by any means."

"And was he . . . shot in the back?"

"How did you know that?"

The bartender came, set down their beers, and went back to the bar.

"Drink your whiskey," Clint said, taking the papers from his pocket, "and then have a look at this."

Roper downed his whiskey, sipped his beer, then accepted the papers from Clint and read each one carefully while Clint sipped his own fresh beer.

TWENTY

"Is this on the level?"

The papers were spread out on the table between them. Clint touched them.

"It seems to be," he said. "Four dead now."

"And what did they have in common?" Roper asked.

"All shot in the back."

"Nothing else?" Roper asked. "What about their finances?"

"None were rich," Clint said, "two were ranchers, one was a drunk, Dolan was . . . a businessman."

"That's right."

"What kind of business?"

"He was a lawyer."

"So he's the first one who was a professional man," Clint said.

"That doesn't help," Roper said. "We need similarities."

"Well," Clint said, "the biggest similarity is that they're all on this list." He tapped it. "Nine men, and one woman."

"There's got to be more," Roper said. "Why don't we go across the street to my office and discuss it further."

"Why not?" Clint said. "Hopefully, the shooter is long gone."

They walked across successfully, without anyone taking a shot at them.

"Where's your new girl?" Clint asked, looking around. The office was empty.

"I don't know," Roper said. "She was here when I left."

"Before the shot?"

Roper looked at Clint.

"Yes."

"How long has she worked for you?"

"Since this morning."

They both walked to her desk. There was no note on the clean desk top.

"This one left even faster than usual," Clint said.

"Too fast," Roper said. "Let's take a look in my office."

"Nothing's missing," Roper said.

"Did you expect that something would be?"

"I don't know," Roper said. "Have a seat. Your problem takes precedence here."

Clint pulled a chair over and sat across from Roper, who seated himself behind his desk.

"Tell me everything you've done, everything you've thought since this all started."

"That might take a while."

"We'll take the time," Roper said, "and then we'll go get some dinner."

"Well, okay. I got the telegram while I was in Labyrinth . . ."

"So you finally decided to take the chance and contact me," Roper said.

"Right."

"And you want to send telegrams to the six remaining people?"

"To them, or someone that you might know, or I might know," Clint said, "but I want the telegrams to come from you. That way I only took one chance, with my telegram to you."

"Which we already know was held up for three days," Roper said.

"It arrived today," Clint said, "and today someone took a shot at you."

"And today," Roper said, "Wendy showed up."

"Wendy, the new girl."

"Come on," Roper said, standing.

"Where to?"

"Something to eat," he said, "but first we're going to visit Mrs. Batchelder."

TWENTY-ONE

Roper walked Clint down the street to another building. On the outside there was a shingle that said, BATCHELDER EMPLOYMENT AGENCY.

"Employment agency?" Clint asked.

"She helps people find jobs," Roper said. "Mostly young ladies."

"Like Wendy."

"That's what I want to find out."

Roper opened the door and they entered.

"Mr. Roper!" a pleasant-looking woman in her fifties cried out. "How nice to see you. Don't tell me you need my talents once again."

"Since this morning, you mean?" he asked.

"This morning?" she asked. "I sent Justine to you three months ago."

"What about Wendy?"

She frowned.

"Wendy?"

"The girl who came to me this morning."

"I didn't send you a girl this morning, Talbot," she said, putting her hands on her hips. "This is upsetting. Is some girl trying to pass herself off as being represented by me?"

"Maybe I misunderstood," Roper said. "I'll talk to her and get back to you."

"Yes, please do," she said, "but meanwhile, do you need someone?"

"Not right now, Mrs. Batchelder," he said, "but as soon as I do, I'll let you know."

"I'll look forward to it," she said. "I have several girls who would be a wonderful fit for you."

"Thank you."

Clint and Roper left the building and stopped just outside.

"This is odd," Roper said.

"If she was sent by my killer," Clint said, "then he already knows that I contacted you. He'll be on his way to his next target—whoever it is."

"Let's have some dinner," Roper said, "and map out a strategy to try to save those other six people."

"Suits me."

"Then we can figure out a way to find out who this killer is."

Roper took Clint to a restaurant he had recently discovered that specialized in steaks. Over two wonderful meals they discussed who they each knew in the next six locations on the list—Minnesota (Grand View), Missouri (Saint Louis), Arizona (Steadfast), South Dakota (White Bluffs), Idaho (Sayerville), and the last one—the woman—in San Francisco.

Roper decided he knew someone he could send to Minnesota, South Dakota, and Idaho. Clint figured he could get someone like Bat Masterson or Luke Short to go to Arizona and Missouri.

"What about San Francisco?" Roper asked over dessert.

"I'm going to San Francisco myself," Clint said. "It's unusual that the last name on the list is a woman. I'm thinking maybe she'll know something helpful about this killer's motives."

"Where would you like me to start?" Roper asked.

"Maybe you could just investigate the murder of Daniel Dolan here in Denver," Clint said. "You might be able to find out something helpful."

"I can do that," Roper said.

"We can both send telegrams tomorrow morning," Clint said. "By midday maybe we can have five of the others covered. I'll get a train to San Francisco tomorrow evening."

"Hopefully, your guy didn't go straight there," Roper said.

"Good point," Clint said. "I wish I could send this woman a telegram—or rather have you send one—but all we have is her name and San Francisco."

"If the shooter today was him—or sent by him—or if he sent the girl to me, then it doesn't matter who sends the telegram, you or me."

"You're right." Clint left his pie half-eaten and sat back. "I suppose I mishandled this whole thing. Four men are dead, and maybe I could have prevented it."

"You certainly could not have prevented that first man from being killed," Roper said. "And you probably did what I would have done."

"I doubt it," Clint said. "You would have come up with a viable alternative after the second killing. So maybe I'm only responsible for the last two deaths—and the next few."

"The person responsible is your killer," Roper said, "and we're going to do whatever we have to do to identify and catch him."

"Thanks, Tal," Clint said. "I appreciate your help."

"Hey," Roper said, "somebody took a shot at me. That's not the kind of thing I take lightly."

"I don't blame you."

They stopped outside the restaurant and shook hands.

"I'll be at your hotel by noon tomorrow," Roper said. "We can compare notes."

Roper had copied the list of names and had that in his pocket. He'd marked off the ones he was supposed to be pursuing. He patted his pocket.

"By then we should have these folks covered."

"I hope so," Clint said. "I hope we can keep another one from being killed."

"I doubt your man could been in Minnesota yet, even if he caught the train last night. We should be able to do this."

"Again, I appreciate your help," Clint said. "Just watch your back, in case the mysterious girl and the shooting today are *not* connected with my killer."

"If somebody from my past chose today to take a run at me, it would be a hell of a coincidence," Roper said.

And Clint knew that Talbot Roper was no more a believer in coincidence than he was.

TWENTY-TWO

Clint returned to the Denver House Hotel, locked the door of his room behind him, and then stuck a chair back beneath the doorknob. If someone had tried to shoot Roper, what would keep them from coming after him?

He took off his jacket and his boots, poured himself a drink from the decanter of brandy the hotel always provided for their regular guests.

He sat in a comfortable armchair and considered the events of the day. Since neither he nor Roper believed in coincidence, the shot taken at Roper had to be connected to the death list. But considering that the killer was a proven back shooter, what was the point of taking a shot at Roper on the street that way? Why not wait until Roper was fitting the key into his office door, his back turned to the street. That would have been a much easier shot to take.

Could the shot have simply been a warning, to both Roper and Clint?

Whatever the reason, Clint was now committed to this

course of action. Try to save the lives of as many of the remaining six people as possible.

He'd rise early in the morning and send his telegrams, and would hopefully get quick responses. If not, he'd have to hope for a response in San Francisco by the time he arrived there.

He finished his drink and then went into the bedroom part of his suite to get more comfortable.

Talbot Roper returned to his office after dinner with Clint, rather than going home. He stopped first at the reception desk, sat there for a few moments thinking, then went through some drawers. After that he rose and walked into his office, sat at his own desk. The girl had undoubtedly done some filing while she was there, but who was to say she didn't just dump the files into one drawer, just so it would look as if she'd filed them?

Roper checked the cabinets. He remembered the names on some of the files, and found them to have been inserted in the proper places.

She had come to his office, done his filing, greeted Clint, and then left. So once Clint had arrived, was that all she wanted to know? Did she run back to her master with that information? And had that resulted in the shot being taken at him?

Why a shot at him?

Why not shoot at Clint?

Was it a warning?

If so, if it was meant as a warning, Talbot Roper did not respond to warnings.

Not favorably anyway.

* * *

Roper knew of a place where he could send telegrams, even at a late time. As he prepared to leave his office, though, he decided not to use the front door. He had another exit, one that nobody else knew about. It was a stairway that took him down to a tunnel, beneath several buildings, and came out on another street entirely.

He went to the hidden door, which was behind a bookcase. He could tell that the bookcase had not been recently moved, so Wendy—whoever she was—had not found this secret exit.

He opened the door, went down the stairs and along the tunnel, using a candle to light the way. It was damp, and he could hear his own footsteps echoing. When he came to the door at the end, he extinguished the candle and put it aside, so it would be available if he had to come back in this way.

Although he was certain no one knew about this door, he opened it slowly, and stepped out carefully. It was dark out, and with no light behind him, he should be totally hidden from sight. Even if someone was across the street with the rifle, it would not be an easy shot.

He closed the door, then ascended the three steps to the street level.

He paused, looked both ways and across the street before he started walking down the street, fairly certain that he was not in anyone's crosshairs.

Roper knew many private detectives—or private "agents," since they were not all licensed—across the country, and meant to call on the ones he knew he could depend on the most. Also, the ones who were geographically located so that they could get to Minnesota, South Dakota, and Idaho as quickly as possible.

He had a friend who would give him access to a private telegraph key, so that he could get his messages off tonight. The sooner he could get in touch with those agents, the better.

TWENTY-THREE

Clint awoke the next morning and went down to talk to the hotel manager. He knew that the hotel had a telegraph key they made available to certain guests—mostly businessmen. But Clint was enough of a regular guest that he felt sure they'd let him use it.

"Of course, sir," the manager said in his office. He hurriedly got up from behind his desk. "Please, follow me."

Clint did so, following the smaller man down a long hallway to a small room with a man sitting at a desk.

"This is our key operator, Jimmy," he said, and the older man got to his feet. "Jimmy, this is Mr. Clint Adams. He has some emergency telegrams he'd like sent."

"Adams," Jimmy said. "Oh, yes, of course, sir. You can write them out here . . ."

"Thank you."

"I'll leave you in Jimmy's hands," the manager said.

"That's fine," Clint said.

As the manager left, Jimmy asked, "Um, how many telegrams will you be sendin'?"

"I'm not sure," Clint said. "That depends on how quickly I get a reply—or not. Let's get started."

Clint ended up sending half a dozen telegrams before he finally got a reply from Bat Masterson.

"Bat Masterson!" Jimmy said, handing him the reply. "Geez."

Masterson said he could make the ride to Saint Louis and check on a man there named Micah Wallace. He said he'd telegraph Clint in San Francisco when he knew something.

"Okay," Clint said to Jimmy, "thanks."

"What about your other ones?" Jimmy asked. "The ones you sent to Luke Short?"

"Well, hopefully I'll get a reply from him while I'm in San Francisco."

"I hope so, sir."

Clint slapped the older man on the back and said, "Thank you, Jimmy."

"You leavin' Denver now?"

"First train I can get," Clint said.

"Have a nice trip."

Clint gave the man a little salute and headed for the lobby, where, at noon, he expected to meet Talbot Roper.

Roper got to the Denver House early, took up position in the lobby so that he'd be able to see Clint as soon as he came down the stairs, and vice versa.

"You're early," Clint said, coming up behind him.

Roper turned quickly and asked, "Where did you come from?"

"Hotel has its own telegraph key," Clint said. "I was using it. How about you?"

"I have a friend with access to a key," Roper said. "I got it all done last night."

"Well, I've got Bat Masterson on his way to Saint Louis," Clint said.

"I've got men on their way to Minnesota, South Dakota, and Idaho."

"Detectives?"

"One of them is licensed, the other two are just . . . let's call them agents. They're good men. If the people on that list are still alive when my men arrive, they'll stay alive."

"What about Arizona?"

"I've reached out to Luke Short," Clint said. "Should hear from him soon."

"When are you leaving for San Francisco?" Roper asked.

"I'm checking out now," Clint said. "I'm going to catch the first train I can."

"I'll go to the station with you to watch your back," the detective said.

"And who's going to watch yours after I leave?" Clint asked.

"Don't worry," Roper said. "I think you should worry more about your back once you're on the train."

Clint thought that his friend was probably right.

Roper went to his suite with him to pick up his saddle-bags and rifle, and then they rode to the station together in a cab.

"I've got one favor to ask you," Clint said on the way.

"One favor?"

"Okay, one more favor," Clint said. "I'm leaving Eclipse at the Denver House livery. Will you look after him for me?"

"Definitely," Roper said. "I know how much that animal means to you. I'll look in on him daily."

"I appreciate it."

When they got to the station, Roper walked in with Clint and waited while he checked on trains.

"There's one leaving in an hour and forty minutes," Clint said. "I got a ticket."

"I'll wait with you."

"You don't have to."

"I've got nothing else to do right now," Roper said. "Besides, I'll feel better once I know you're safely on the train."

"Then what are you going to do?" Clint asked.

"Two things," Roper said. "I'm going to find this girl, Wendy. And I'll find out as much as I can about the murder of Daniel Dolan."

"Okay, keep me informed about all that."

"Where are you going to stay?"

"A friend of mine just opened a hotel near Portsmouth Square called the Lucky Strike. I'll be staying there."

"The Lucky Strike. Got it."

Roper walked Clint right onto the train, then stood on the platform while the train pulled away.

Clint watched his friend fade into the distance, then sat back in his seat. Hopefully, he could relax until he got to San Francisco.

But in reality, he never relaxed, no matter where he was. That was simply what it meant to be Clint Adams.

TWENTY-FOUR

Clint was impressed with the Lucky Strike. He knew several people with hotels near Portsmouth Square, the gambling center of San Francisco. This one was brand new, and he could see the money that his friend, Kenny "King" Dirker, had put into it. King Dirker was a great poker player who had decided to stop playing and become the House. He did that because the House never lost. And the Lucky Strike was now his house.

Clint walked into the impressive lobby and approached the desk. The clerk looked at him with an attitude. He saw a man with saddlebags and a rifle, and no luggage.

"Sir?" he asked with his nose in the air.

"Clint Adams," he said. "You have a room for me."

"Do we?"

"Yes," Clint said, "you do."

The clerk took a moment to check his register, then looked surprised and said, "Oh, yes, we do."

"I'll take my key," Clint said.

"Sir, we can—"

"And tell Kenny I'm here."

"Kenny?"

"Yes, your boss, King Dirker."

"Um, you know Mr. Dirker?"

"Yes, I know Mr. Dirker very well. Mr. Dirker is expecting me. Please tell him that I'm here."

"Uh, yes, sir," the clerk said with a changing attitude. "I will let him know."

Clint put his hand out for his key. The clerk grabbed it from the wall behind him and placed it in Clint's palm.

"Room fifteen, sir," the clerk said. "One of our best rooms."

"Thank you."

Clint closed his hand around the key, took his rifle and saddlebags, and climbed the stairs to the second floor.

Clint was still being impressed with his suite when there was knock on the door. He opened it, hand on his gun, and saw King Dirker standing in the hall.

"Clint!"

Dirker was a big man. He bull-rushed Clint, grabbed him in a bear hug, and lifted him off the floor. "How the hell are ya?"

"I'd be better if you stopped squeezing the life out of me."

Dirker put Clint down and released him.

"What do you think of the place?"

"It's beautiful," Clint said. "A beautiful place." He looked around the suite at the plush furniture and draperies. "If I didn't know better, I'd think I was smack in the center of Portsmouth Square."

"I know! It's great, isn't it?" Dirker frowned. "That little weasel at the front desk give you any problems?"

"No, just a little bit of an attitude."

"Yeah, I'm gonna fire his ass sooner or later," Dirker said. "Problem is the little peckerwood is good at his job."

"Well, then, don't fire him on my account," Clint said.

"Look here," Dirker said, walking to a sidebar, which had several crystal decanters on it. "The good stuff. Whataya have?"

"I'd rather check out your saloon and have a beer."

"You got it!" Dirker said, "Come on, let's go."

They left the suite and went back down to the main floor.

"Come 'ere a minute," Dirker said, and pulled Clint over to the front desk.

The clerk saw his boss coming toward him and straightened his back.

"Sir!"

"Listen, you little peckerwood," Dirker said, "this is Clint Adams, one of my best friends in the world. You give him whatever he wants, you get me?"

"Yessir."

"I don't care what it is."

"Yessir."

"King, come on—" Clint said.

"You understand me?" Dirker said to the clerk.

"Yessir, I do."

"Come on, King," Clint said. "I need a beer."

Dirker allowed himself to be drawn away from the desk, then took the lead and marched Clint into the saloon and right up to the bar. The place was all gold and mahogany, and it all shined brightly.

At the bar Dirker yelled, "Two beers!"

The bartender took a look, saw his boss, and said, "Comin' up."

Clint looked around. The place was empty, but he was sure the casino was jumping.

"Come on," Dirker said, "I keep a table in the back."

Clint followed Dirker to his table, and sat across from him.

"Okay," Dirker said, "I got your telegram. Tell me what's going on."

"It's a long story, and kind of hard to believe," Clint said.

"Don't worry," Dirker said, "I'll keep the beer coming."

And he did . . .

TWENTY-FIVE

Clint gave Dirker the whole story, removing the folded papers from his pocket and handing them over.

"This sounds too incredible," he said when Clint had finished.

"I know it."

"I think you did the right thing bringin' in Roper and Bat," Dirker said.

"I'm waiting to hear from Luke Short if he can help," Clint said. "Otherwise I'll have to find somebody else."

"To go where?"

"Arizona."

"I've got somebody," Dirker said. "I'll get ahold of him today." Dirker checked the list. "I'll put him on this guy Kevin Lockerby."

"Do you know any of the other names on that list?" Clint asked.

Dirker looked again. As Clint watched him read, he saw a flash of recognition spread across his face.

"Jesus," he said, "what is she doin' on this list?"

"You know the woman?"

"Everybody in San Francisco knows this woman. It's Amanda Tolliver."

"You mean I could have sent her a telegram from Denver and it would have reached her?"

"Maybe," Dirker said. "She has bodyguards, people you have to go through before you can see her. No telling how long it would have taken for a telegram to get to her."

"Can I get to her personally?"

"Maybe . . . if she finds you interesting."

"Who is she?"

"The wife of a very powerful man," Dirker said, "and he doesn't let just anyone see her."

"How do I get to her, then? Through him? Wouldn't he like to know that his wife's life is in danger?"

"I'm thinkin' . . ."

"What?"

"He probably would want to know, unless . . ."

"Unless what?" Clint asked. "Come on, King, spit it out."

"Well, her husband is Ben Tolliver. He's a powerful man in publishing and politics in San Francisco. He's also been known to . . . get rid of people who go against him."

"Are you telling me he'd arrange to have his own wife killed?"

Dirker shrugged. "If she was in his way, he might."

"So I can't go to him," Clint said. "I've got to get right to her."

"That'd be your best bet."

"And how do I do that?"

"Well," Dirker said, "you two have somethin' in common."

"What's that?"

"Gambling."

"What does she play?"

"A little of everything, but she likes cards. Blackjack, faro . . . and poker."

"Have you played her?"

"No."

"Has she played here?"

"No, we're too new," Dirker said. "She plays at the more established houses in the Square."

"When?"

"Every night."

"Then I guess I'm going to Portsmouth Square tonight."

"You'll have to get past her bodyguards."

"I don't mean her any harm."

"It doesn't matter," Dirker said. "Her husband pays them to keep men away from her."

Clint considered the problem.

"What were you saying about getting her interested?" he asked.

"Well," Dirker said, "I guess if you were to beat her at her own game . . . she hates to lose."

"And would that get her interested, or mad at me?" Clint asked.

Dirker shrugged.

"Maybe they're the same."

"Is she any good?"

"She's very good."

"At which game?"

"All of them."

"What does she like the best?"

"Well . . . like I said, cards, and she's also said to like . . . men."

"She's married to a powerful man, and cheats on him?" Clint asked.

"Like I said," Dirker replied, "the lady likes to gamble."

TWENTY-SIX

Clint and Dirker split up in the lobby. Dirker told him he'd telegraph his man in Arizona, and get back to Clint as soon as he knew something.

Meanwhile, Clint needed some clothes that would keep him from standing out in Portsmouth Square. He did not want to attract anyone's attention but that of Amanda Tolliver.

Clint thought about going out shopping, but then got a better idea. He went to the desk, where the same desk clerk watched him nervously.

"What's your name?"

"Laurence, sir."

"I'm going to call you Larry," Clint said.

The man looked pained but said, "Very well, sir."

"Larry, I need a good tailor to come to my room, measure me for a suit, and have it done by tonight."

"Sir, that's almost . . . impossible."

"But I heard your boss tell you to get me anything I want."

"Well, yes, sir, but—"

"Do you know a good tailor?"

"Well, yes, sir."

"That's the first step. Can you get him here?"

"Yes."

"Step two. Do that, and I'll take it from there."

"Yessir."

"I'll be in my room . . . waiting."

"Yes, sir."

Half an hour later there was a knock at his door. He opened it, hand on his gun, to find a man in a white shirt with a measuring tape around his neck. There was another man with him, younger, his arms loaded with bolts of cloth.

"You needed a suit, sir?"

"Yes," Clint said, "tonight."

"Then we should get started, sir."

Clint hesitated, looking the two men over. "Come on in," he said finally, backing away.

The tailor and his assistant entered.

"Stop there."

They stopped.

"Drop that stuff on the floor," he told the younger man.

"On the floor?" the boy asked.

"Yes."

The assistant looked at the tailor, who nodded. He dropped the bolts to the ground. Clint poked at them with his foot, spreading them all out. No weapons.

"Either of you carrying a gun?" he asked.

"I'm a tailor," the man said, "not a gunfighter."

The young man said, "Not me."

Clint looked them both up and down, saw that there was no point in searching them.

"Okay. Go ahead, pick them up."

The boy picked up the cloth and stood there holding them again.

"We need to get started," the tailor said, "if you want to have that suit by tonight."

"That's right."

"It won't be cheap."

"Don't worry about it."

"I'll have to measure you."

"I understand."

"Without the gun."

Clint removed his holster, hung it on the back of a chair, then stood next to the chair.

"What's your name?" he asked the tailor.

"John."

"John, I need a suit to go to Portsmouth Square with, and I don't want to stand out."

"Understood. What color?"

"It doesn't matter," Clint said. "Whatever you got there. Blue? Gray? Black?"

"Let's go with blue," the tailor said. "Spread your legs, sir."

"Clint," Clint said, "my name's Clint."

He spread his legs.

The tailor knew his job, quickly took Clint's measurements, and left with them.

"I'll have the suit delivered this evening," he said.

"Thanks."

As the tailor was leaving with his assistant, Dirker showed up.

"Mr. Dirker," the tailor said.

"John."

Dirker came in and closed the door behind him.

"You get that telegram sent to Arizona?" Clint asked.

"I did," Dirker said. "My man is on his way."

"Any telegrams for me?"

"No."

"I guess that's good, and bad."

"How so?"

"If Roper had any news about those other names, he would've telegraphed me. That'd be bad, so it's good. And if Luke Short had gotten any of my telegrams, he would've answered. That would've been good, so that's bad."

Dirker shook his head and said, "I don't know what you just said, but my man's on the way, so you won't need Short."

"I hope you're right."

Dirker changed the subject.

"John's a good tailor. You'll have a suit to go gamblin' in tonight."

"Well, then, I guess I better get myself some rest," Clint said. "I'll want to be at my best when I meet the lady."

"Don't forget what I said," Dirker told him. "You'll have to make her interested in you."

"Well, when it comes to women, I haven't ever had much trouble."

"My friend," Dirker said, "you ain't never met a woman like this before."

"Well, King," Clint said, "now you've made *me* interested."

TWENTY-SEVEN

The next time Clint answered the door, the tailor's assistant was standing there, holding a suit.

"The tailor didn't come?"

"H-He said it'd fit. There was no need for him to come."

"Come on in."

"Y-You want me to wait?"

"I do."

The boy entered, stood there nervously.

"Let me have the suit. I'll go in the other room and try it on."

The boy handed it over.

"Now just wait there until I come out."

"Yessir."

"If it fits, I'll pay you and you can take the money to your boss."

"Yessir."

Clint went into the bedroom to try the suit on. When he came out, the boy was still standing there.

"It fits," Clint said. "You got a bill for me?"

"Yessir."

He took a piece of paper from his pocket and handed it to Clint.

"Well," Clint said, looking at it, "he was right."

"About w-what?"

"It sure ain't cheap."

Clint sent the boy back to the tailor with his money. He grabbed up his Colt New Line, stuck it in the back of his belt, then put on his hat. Briefly, he wished he'd taken the time to buy a new one, one that matched the suit. He'd just have to take this one off when he got to the casino.

He went downstairs to have a beer in the hotel's saloon first, and to check out Dirker's gambling setup before he went to Portsmouth Square.

"Well, look at you," Dirker said in the lobby. "Ain't you pretty."

"Cost a pretty penny, so I better be pretty in it," Clint said.

"Wait for me in the bar," Dirker said.

"What for?"

"Just do it. Have a beer in the house."

"That I'll do."

Clint went into the saloon, and up to the bar.

"Beer," he said to the bartender, "and your boss is on the way, so you better make it two."

"Comin' up."

When Dirker appeared, there was a beer waiting for him on the bar.

"Here," he said, handing Clint a brand-new black Stetson.

"The suit's blue," Clint said.

"Don't worry about it," Dirker said. "This one goes better with the suit than that worn-out thing. Give it to the bartender. He'll hold it for you, in case you want it back."

Clint handed the bartender his hat and tried on the new one. He looked at himself in the mirror behind the bar.

"Not bad."

"Yeah," Dirker said, "you're real pretty now. Look like you belong in the Alhambra."

"Hell," Clint said, "the Bella Union, the Empire, the Arcade . . . which one does she gamble at?"

"You'll have to hit them all until you find her," Dirker said. "Start at Sam Dennison's Exchange and the Parker House. And there's no guarantee you'll run into her the first night."

"Damn it, King," Clint said, "I need to see her right away to warn her. And to find out if she knows anything."

"Well, you could go to her house."

"You know where that is?"

"I do."

"Why didn't you tell me that in the beginning?" Clint demanded.

"Well, about the only people who actually get to go into that house are the mayor, some other politicians, and some businessmen—and I mean the men who run things."

"Damn it," Clint said. "Okay, I'll try the Square first tonight, but if I don't see her, I'm going to have to try the house tomorrow. What about her husband's office?"

"Market Street," Dirker said, "but same problem. Ya got to be somebody to get in."

"Well," the bartender said, speaking for the first time, "he's the Gunsmith, ain't he? Don't that make him somebody?"

Dirker scratched his cheek and said to Clint, "He might have a point, you know."

Clint headed for the door, then turned and asked, "What does she look like?"

"Oh," Dirker said, "you'll know her when you see her."

TWENTY-EIGHT

Clint did as King Dirker suggested, he started at the Parker House, then moved on to the Exchange. After that the Bella Union, the Verandah, the Aguila de Oro, the Varsouvienne, and the Mazourka.

It was late, and he was about to quit when he got to the Alhambra, one of the oldest establishments in San Francisco. If he didn't find her there, there were still plenty of places to try the next night. That is, if he couldn't get to her or her husband during the day.

The Alhambra was in full swing, with only one of the tables showing any room at the moment. But that one seemed to have attracted more attention than the others.

Women who gambled usually attracted some attention. Clint had known more than one. Poker Alice, Lottie Deno, Big Nosed Kate, Kitty Leroy. But a beautiful woman who gambled—well, she attracted crowds. He had the feeling that when Dirker said he'd know Amanda Tolliver, he meant that she was beautiful.

Maybe he was about to find out.

* * *

The dealer had never had this many people watch him deal before. His hands were sweating.

"Goddamn it, dealer," one of the gamblers said, "you're makin' the cards clammy. Get a new deck."

"Yes, sir," the dealer said.

On top of all the people making him nervous, he also had Amanda Tolliver at his table. That really made him nervous.

"What's your name?"

He looked up. She was actually speaking to him.

"Ma'am?"

"Your name."

"Billy."

"What's making you so nervous, Billy?" she asked.

"Well, ma'am," he said as he opened a new deck, "I ain't never had this many people watch me deal, and I sure as hel—heck ain't never had no woman as pretty as you at my table."

"Oh, Billy," she said, fluttering her eyes at him, "you flatter me."

The dealer blushed.

"Don't be talkin' to the lady like that," one of the men standing behind her told him.

She looked up at her two bodyguards.

"Oh, shut up, Hawkins," she told the speaker. "He's just stating a fact, not trying to bed the boss's wife."

"Ma'am, I'm just—"

"Be quiet, I said." She looked at Billy. "Just concentrate on dealing the cards, Billy. Forget the people, and forget about me, and your hands won't sweat so much."

"Yes, ma'am. I'll try."

There were four other players at the table, all men, and none of them had spoken to her all night, unless it had to do with their cards. They all knew who she was, and while their hands weren't sweating as much as the dealer's, her presence made them nervous.

There was still one empty seat at the table, where a player had busted out earlier.

"Cards are comin' out," the dealer said. "Five-card stud."

"Hell, sonny," one of the players said, "that's what we been playin' all night. Just deal 'em."

"Yes, sir," Billy said. "Comin' out."

TWENTY-NINE

Clint moved to the fringes of the crowd and started working his way in. Finally, he got close enough that he could
see who was at the table. There were four men and a
woman playing, and a dealer.

And an empty seat.

The woman had red hair piled high on her head and
a long, graceful, pale neck that swooped down into an
impressive bosom. He couldn't see her eyes, because she
was looking down at her cards.

He also saw the two broad-shouldered men standing
behind her, their eyes looking everywhere but at her. Hell,
if he had been standing where they were, he would have
been looking right down the front of her dress.

One of them caught his eyes and stared at him hard.
Clint smiled at him.

He watched the hand play out, was impressed with
how cool she was, even though she lost it.

"Is that chair open?" he asked.

All eyes turned to him, including those of the lady.

They were green and he caught his breath when he saw her face.

"It certainly is," she said, "and we could use some new blood."

"Ma'am—" her bodyguard said.

"Shut up, Hawkins," she said again. "The man just wants to play cards."

Hawkins closed his mouth, but he wasn't happy. He glared at Clint as he worked his way around the table and sat down.

"This is a high-stakes game, sir," the dealer said.

"I think my marker will be good."

"I'll have to call my boss."

"Do it."

"Can I tell him your name?"

"Clint Adams."

A murmur went through the crowd. He looked across the table at the woman he assumed was Amanda Tolliver and thought he saw interest in her eyes.

Mission accomplished? he wondered.

Meanwhile, the dealer's eyes widened and he said to Clint, "No, that's all right, sir. I'm sure your marker will be good."

The dealer passed Clint the chips he'd need to play.

"Cards," the dealer said.

The word spread that the Gunsmith was playing poker. The bartender at the Lucky Strike was correct. He was enough of a somebody to draw attention—but it was too much attention. He had gone about it the wrong way. He never should have used his real name.

But it was too late to change it now.

He played for two hours, and the cards were coming. Two of the other players busted out of the game, and nobody else sat down.

"Mr. Adams," the woman said to him, "you certainly have changed the complexion of this game since you sat down."

"Is that good or bad, ma'am?"

"I say it's good," she replied. "I was getting . . . bored."

"Then I'm glad I could accommodate you, ma'am."

"Oh my God, stop calling me ma'am," she said. "You're the only man at this table who's dared to speak to me all night. My name is Amanda, Amanda Tolliver."

"Pleased to meet you, Miss Tolliver," he said.

"That's Mrs. Tolliver," one of her bodyguards said. It was not the one she called Hawkins. He had probably gotten tired of being told to shut up.

"Oh, sorry," Clint said. "Mrs. Tolliver."

"If this game goes on another couple hours," she said, "I may let you call me Amanda."

"Mrs. Tolliver—"

"Shut up, Hawkins!"

THIRTY

The game came down to Amanda and Clint, and the two bodyguards standing behind her. The crowd began to spread out as it got later and later.

"Looks like people are losing interest, Mr. Adams," she said.

"My name is Clint, Mrs. Tolliver."

She stared across the table at him and mouthed "Amanda" at him, so her bodyguards couldn't see. He smiled at her.

"Looks like we're evenly matched," she said. They had taken everyone else's chips.

"For tonight anyway," Clint said.

"Mrs. Tolliver . . ." the bodyguard who wasn't Hawkins said.

She sighed and said, "All right, Max."

Clint wondered why he was Max, but the other man was always "Hawkins."

"Clint, it's time for me to go home and be a responsible wife."

"Too bad," Clint said.

They each tossed the dealer a chip and thanked him.

"Amanda," Clint said as the dealer stood up and left, "I need to talk to you for a few minutes."

"Really?" she asked. "About what?"

"I actually came out to the casinos tonight looking for you."

"I'm flattered."

"Mrs. Tolliver—" Max said.

"Max, why don't you take Hawkins to the bar and buy him a drink?"

"Ma'am—"

"I'm not going anywhere," she said. "I swear. The Gunsmith wants to talk to me. Is that something you think I should pass up?"

"Ma'am, your husband said—"

"He wants you to keep me alive and safe," she said. "You can do that from the bar."

Max looked dubious, but finally he pushed Hawkins ahead of him and they walked to the bar.

"Well, since we have to wait for our chips to be cashed in, go ahead and talk—if that's what you really want to do."

"Somebody is planning to kill you," he said.

She stared at him for a few moments.

"Maybe I need Max and Hawkins again?"

"No, listen to me," Clint said. "This is important. It's why I came here looking for you."

"The casinos?"

"To San Francisco."

"You came to San Francisco looking for me?" she asked. "Why?"

"Because your name is on a list," he said, "and the first four names on that list are dead men."

She stared at him and asked, "Is this for a real? Or a way to get to my husband through me?"

"It's real," he said. "I have the list in my pocket."

"And . . . what number am I on that list?"

"Ten," he said. "Last."

"Let me see it."

He took the list out of his pocket and handed it to her. Seeing this, both Max and Hawkins came striding over.

"What's goin' on?" Max asked.

She didn't answer. She was staring at the list.

"Amanda?" Clint said.

"Mrs. Tolliver," Max said, "it's time to go."

"Yes," she said, "yes, of course." She put the list down on the table and stood up.

"Amanda—" Clint said, standing up.

Max and Hawkins got between Clint and Amanda.

"Don't try it, friend," Max said.

"But Amanda—"

"Good-bye, Mr. Adams," she said, and headed for the door.

Clint started forward, but Max laid a big hand on his chest.

"No," the big bodyguard said.

Hawkins, who was even bigger, just shook his head, and then they turned and followed her out.

Clint thought about following to force the issue, but decided against it. From the look on her face, she had recognized some of the names on the list. She was either going to go home and talk to her husband, or she'd find a way to contact him for more information—maybe without her bodyguards around.

Also, she'd have to come back sometime to pick up the cash from her chips.

He cashed out and left to go back to the Lucky Strike Casino.

THIRTY-ONE

It was 1:30 a.m. when Amanda got back to the house she shared with her husband on Telegraph Hill.

As she entered their bedroom, she found him sitting in his favorite armchair. There was a book in his lap and a glass of brandy on the table next to him.

"Did you win?"

"Of course."

He set the book aside with a satisfied smile. He watched as she undressed. She was three decades younger than him. She had a flawless body, high, firm breasts, wide hips, pale skin. She approached him naked, got on her knees in front of him, and parted his robe. She took his flaccid penis in her hands.

"I played five-card stud most of the night, beating all the boys," she said as she manipulated and stroked him.

"That's good. And did Max and Hawkins behave?"

"They did fine," she said.

She leaned forward and kissed his penis, licked the head. When she finally took it in her mouth, it began to swell. She stroked it some more, parted the robe even farther so she could get to his balls. As she licked his cock and fondled his balls, he became harder and harder. This was not the price she had to pay for going out to gamble without him; it was his reward for letting her go.

His cock was finally hard and swollen with blood. She sucked it wetly, taking it all the way into her mouth, moaning as she bobbed up and down on it. Finally, she stood, straddled him, reached down to take hold of him and guide him to her wet portal. She sat down on him, took his cock deep inside, and began to rock in his lap.

"Oh, yes," he said, "that's it, my sweet . . ."

She went from rocking back and forth to bouncing up and down on him while he gasped and groped at her breasts.

It didn't take long before he was jetting inside her. She moaned and groaned and made a big deal of it, telling him what a man he was and how she loved him. She climbed off him and stood in front of him with his juices sliding down her thighs.

"I need to take a bath," she said.

"Of course, darling," he said. He closed his robe and picked up his book again. "I'll be right here, waiting to go to bed."

"I won't be long," she said, saying nothing to him about meeting Clint Adams, nothing to him about the list Adams had shown her.

She had a lot of thinking to do in the bath.

In the hot bath she thought about Clint Adams and the list he had shown her. She had recognized not only some of the names on that list, but all of them. They were all people who had done business with her husband at one time or another. In some cases her husband had ruined them.

Who would have made such a list, and then started killing them off one by one? And put her last on that list? If it was someone with a grudge against her husband, why not put him last?

But no, someone with a grudge against Ben Tolliver would not go out and start killing off his past business conquests. That was an oddity. That was something she could not even see Ben doing himself. Why would he? What would be the point?

And if somebody made a list like that, why in the world would he bring it to the attention of a man like the Gunsmith?

None of this made sense.

THIRTY-TWO

It was 2 a.m. when Clint found Dirker working his own casino. The Lucky Strike was no Alhambra, but it was an impressive layout, nevertheless, and was obviously doing well for an establishment that had opened very recently.

"You're back," Dirker said when he saw Clint. He spread his arms. "Whataya think?"

"Very nice, King," Clint said. "You've done well for yourself."

"Even better than you think," Dirker said. "I got the word from my guy in Arizona that your man there is still alive."

"That's good," Clint said.

"How did your evening go?"

"Pretty well," Clint said. "I won some money playing poker."

"You played? I thought you were just gonna look for the lady in question."

"Well," Clint said, "when I got to the Alhambra, the lady in question was already playing poker, so I sat in."

"You played with her?" Dirker said. "Let's go get a beer so you can tell me about it."

Minutes later they were seated at Dirker's table in the saloon, each with a beer. Clint told Dirker about playing in the game, and meeting Amanda Tolliver and her two bodyguards.

"Did you get a chance to talk to her?" the hotel owner asked. "Tell her what was going on?"

"I did," Clint said. "I showed her the list."

"And?"

"She froze. I think she recognized at least some of the names on the list."

"You didn't ask her about it?"

"That was when she decided to leave and her bodyguards got between us."

"And you let her go?"

"If she knows some of those names, I think she'll find a way for us to talk without her bodyguards around, don't you?"

"I suppose," Dirker said, "unless . . ."

"Unless what?"

"Unless she just goes home and talks about it with her husband."

"I don't think she'll do that."

"Why not?"

"The lady strikes me as having a mind of her own."

"I don't know," Dirker said. "He is said to have a hard hold on her."

"We'll see," Clint said.

Dirker leaned forward and lowered his voice.

"You really think she'll try to see you?"

"I hope so."

"What did you think of her?"

"She's a decent poker player."

"And?"

"And a beautiful woman."

"And?"

"A beautiful women who has two big bodyguards around her at all times."

"If you'd really wanted to continue talking to her, you wouldn't have let that stop you," Dirker said. "I know you."

"You're right," Clint said. "She was shocked by that list. I'm going to wait for the shock to wear off, and then she'll come looking for me."

"You hope."

"I hope."

They finished their beer and then Dirker invited Clint to gamble in the Lucky Strike.

"Your marker's always good with me."

"If I was going to gamble, I'd use the money I won tonight at the Alhambra."

"I like the sound of that."

"Maybe tomorrow," Clint said. "I'm beat—still from traveling, and then from trolling Portsmouth Square most of the evening and playing poker most of the night."

"Who were the other players?" Dirker asked as they reentered the lobby of the hotel.

"I don't know," Clint said. "They barely spoke. In fact, Amanda said I was the only man who had spoken to her all night."

"Oh, it's Amanda, is it?"

"Oh yeah," Clint said. "We got on a first-name basis and were doing very well until I showed her that list."

"I'm going to be very interested to hear what she has to say about it."

"I am, too."

THIRTY-THREE

In the morning Amanda told her husband at breakfast that she wanted to do some shopping.

"That's fine," he said. "I have to go into the office myself. Just make sure you take Max and Hawkins with you."

"Do I have to?" she asked.

"Amanda," he said, sternly, "we've discussed this before."

"They scare the other women who are shopping," she complained.

"They're just doing their jobs, dear."

"How about this," she said. "I'll just take one of them with me. Maybe one won't scare the women that much."

Tolliver considered the request.

"Please, Benny," she said. She knew he liked it when she called him "Benny." Nobody else did. Nobody else was allowed.

"Oh, all right," he said. "Take one of them. You choose which one."

"Thank you, dear," she said with satisfaction. "More coffee?"

Clint went down to the hotel dining room for breakfast, found King Dirker already there. The hotel owner waved him over, at the same time waving over a waiter.

"Bring my friend steak and eggs," he told the waiter, "and make it a big steak."

"Yes, sir."

Clint sat down, righted one of the cups on the table, and poured himself a cup of coffee.

"How'd you sleep?" Dirker asked.

"Great," Clint said truthfully. "The bed is great."

"Good to hear."

"Any telegrams today?"

"I knew you'd ask," Dirker said, and handed Clint two of them.

The first was from Bat Masterson in Saint Louis. All was well there—the man on the list was alive and well and Bat was going to keep him that way.

The second was from Roper. The men in Idaho and South Dakota were okay, but the man in Minnesota was dead. Roper's agent could not get there in time.

"That's five," Clint said, shaking his head.

"So you'll save the other five," Dirker said, "including Mrs. Tolliver."

"I hope so," Clint said. "I hope I'm right about her coming here to find me. Otherwise I'm going to have to try to find her again."

"That'll mean going through her husband and her bodyguards," Dirker said. "That won't be easy—but you'll find a way."

* * *

Clint and Dirker were working on their breakfasts when the desk clerk—one Clint had not seen before—came into the dining room and approached the table.

"What is it, Lou?" Dirker asked.

This man was older than the other clerk and had a lot less attitude.

"There's a woman at the desk askin' for Mr. Adams," he said.

"Did she give her name?" Clint asked.

"No, sir," Lou said, "but I recognize her. It's Mrs. Tolliver."

Dirker looked at Clint.

"Where do you want to do this?"

"I guess that'll depend on where she wants to do it," Clint said, "but why don't we try in here for now?"

Dirker looked at the clerk and said, "Show the lady in here."

"Yessir."

Dirker waved frantically at the waiter as the clerk left.

"Sir?"

"A fresh pot of coffee, fast!"

"Yessir."

The waiter made a beeline for the kitchen and returned with a fresh pot just as Lou appeared at the door, leading Amanda Tolliver.

"Now go!" Dirker told the waiter.

Clint and Dirker both stood as Amanda reached them.

"Mrs. Tolliver," Clint said, "how nice. Let me introduce Kenny Dirker, he's—"

"King Dirker," she said, extending her hand to the hotel owner. "I know who you are, sir. I've seen you play poker."

"I'm flattered," Dirker said. "Also flattered to have you in my place."

"I came to speak with Mr. Adams," she said. "Would it insult you if I asked to speak to him alone?"

"Not at all," Dirker said. "I'll leave you to it. I have some work to do." He looked at Clint. "I'll see you later."

As Dirker left, Clint pulled out another chair and held it for Amanda.

"Can I get you anything?" he asked.

"No, I've had breakfast," she said. "I could use some coffee, though."

"This is a fresh pot," he said.

He poured her a cup and pushed it over to him. She looked around, as if searching the room to see if there was anyone she knew. Clint figured even if there wasn't, there were bound to be some people there who knew her.

"Where are your bodyguards today?"

"I convinced my husband to let me go shipping with just one," she said. "Hawkins. I lost him in a dress shop."

"Sounds like somebody's going to get fired."

"Probably," she said, "but I don't really like Hawkins."

"I got that feeling last night."

"Yes, I'm here about last night, Mr. Adams."

"Clint, please."

"All right, Clint," she said. "It's about that list you showed me."

"I thought it might," he said. "It looked to me like you recognized some of the names."

"Clint," she said, "that's the problem. I recognized all of the names."

THIRTY-FOUR

"Well," Clint said, "that's . . . interesting."

She was still looking the room over.

"Do you want to go someplace else?" he asked.

"No," she said, "this is as good as any. I'm sure Hawkins is looking for me frantically."

"Do you want to tell me about the names on the list?" he asked. "By the way, I just got the word today. Five of them are dead."

"Oh my God," she said, "how?"

"Shot in the back."

"This is crazy."

"I agree."

"Who could be doing this?"

"I was hoping you'd be able to tell me that," Clint said.

"I don't know," she said.

"Then maybe you can tell me what all these people have in common?"

"All I can see," she said, "is that, at one time or another, they did business with my husband."

"How do you know that?"

"We've been married for ten years," she said. "He's quite a bit older than me, married me when I was nineteen. I recognize all these names from the past ten years."

"You know that much about your husband's business?"

"Yes."

"So then why are you on this list?"

"I can't tell you that," she said. "I don't know."

"Could it be possible that your husband made this list?"

She sat back in her chair. She was wearing a very sedate-looking suit, probably what women wore in San Francisco when they went shopping.

"If I wasn't on the list, I'd say it could be possible."

"But why would he do it?" Clint asked. "Why would your husband want these men killed?"

"I don't know."

"Why would he want you killed?"

"He wouldn't," she said firmly.

"Are you sure?"

"Yes."

"Everything in the marriage is all right?"

"That's an impertinent question."

"Sorry," he said, "but I'm trying to save the lives of the last five people on this list—and that includes you."

"Why?" she asked. "Why are you interested? How did you get involved?"

He explained the situation to her while they each had another cup of coffee. The remainder of Clint's excellent breakfast had gone cold on the plate, and the waiter had come to claim it.

"Can I see the papers?" she asked. "The list again, the note?"

"Sure." Clint handed them over.

She studied both of them very carefully, then dropped them to the table and shook her head.

"Is that your husband's handwriting?" he asked.

"No."

"You're sure?"

"Yes, I am sure."

"Amanda—Mrs. Tolliver—is having people killed something your husband does in his work?"

She glared at him.

"That question is beyond impertinent," she said. "I think we're done here."

As she stood, Clint said, "Amanda, if you're sure your husband isn't behind this, then he should be told about it."

"Do you want to tell him?"

That surprised him.

"I wouldn't mind—"

"Good. Come to my house tonight. For dinner. You can tell him then."

"Dinner?"

"Give me something to write on."

He gave her one of the telegrams he'd received that morning. She hurriedly wrote down her address.

"Be there at seven," she said, "and wear the suit you wore last night."

"I appreciate it—"

"If you're really trying to save lives, there's no reason why I shouldn't help you," she said.

"Especially since one of the lives may be yours," he reminded her.

"Exactly," she said. "I'll see you tonight, Clint."

He stood.

"Would you like me to get you a cab—"

"The doorman can do it," she said. "I interrupted your breakfast. Have another. I'll pay—"

"That's okay," Clint said. "I know the owner. He'll take care of it."

"Then I'll see you tonight."

She left, winding her way between tables.

Only moments after she left, Dirker came walking back in.

"How did that go?" he asked.

"I'm invited to dinner."

"Tolliver invited you to dinner?"

"Tolliver doesn't know about it yet."

"That'll be interesting. What happened to her bodyguards?"

"She lost them so she could come here."

"That's gonna get somebody fired."

"That's what I said."

Dirker waved down the waiter.

"Bring Mr. Adams another steak and eggs."

"Yessir."

"A smaller steak this time," Clint said.

"Ah, what the hell," Dirker said. "Bring me another one, too."

THIRTY-FIVE

Since the other four names on the list were covered, it was Clint's responsibility to keep Amanda Tolliver alive. At dinner he would first have to convince himself that her husband had nothing to do with the list, and then he'd have to convince the man to let him keep his wife alive.

As far as actually investigating any of the deaths, that was being handled by Roper in Denver, and one of his agents—also a detective—in Minnesota. So Clint was basically going to have to sell himself to Tolliver as a bodyguard. And the way Amanda had given Hawkins the slip that morning, maybe that wouldn't be so hard.

He killed the day in the Lucky Strike, talking with Dirker, doing a little bit of gambling, until it was time for him to go up and put his new suit on again.

"Just as pretty as last night," Dirker said when Clint came down. "I'll have the doorman get you a cab. You got a gun on you?"

"Of course I do."

Dirker looked him up and down.

"That little twenty-five of yours?"

"It'll do the job."

"Only in your hands."

"I'll see you later."

As Clint started for the door, Dirker said, "Come and find me when you get back. I want to hear everything."

Clint nodded and left.

"What's this?" Ben Tolliver asked as he entered the dining room. "Are we having a guest for dinner?"

"We are," Amanda said.

"Who?"

"Clint Adams."

"The man you played poker with last night?" he asked. "The Gunsmith?"

"That's right."

"Why is he coming here?" Tolliver demanded. "I thought it was understood that I invite the people who have dinner here."

"This is different," she said.

"Oh? Why?"

She stopped fussing with the table setting and turned to face her husband.

"He's the man I went to see this morning when I gave Hawkins the slip."

"So it's his fault Hawkins was fired?"

"I suppose you could look at it that way."

"And this man, he interests you?"

"He should interest you," she said.

"And why's that?"

"He had something to tell me, something that interested me and should interest you."

"Yes, yes, you said that," Tolliver pointed out in annoyance. "Spit it out, woman."

"Someone is planning to kill me."

"What? That's ridiculous."

"He was sent a list of ten names," she said. "Nine men and me. The first five men are already dead."

Tolliver frowned.

"Who'd make such a list?"

"That's what he's trying to find out."

"And so he's coming here . . . what? To ask me?"

"To warn us," she said, "and to see if we know anything that would help him."

"Help him to do what?"

"Save the lives of the rest of the men on that list," she said, "and me."

Tolliver frowned again.

"You want him to save me, don't you?"

"I'm not convinced that you are in danger," Tolliver said, "but if you are, I would certainly welcome any help in protecting you."

"Good," she said. "He'll be here at seven. You might want to change for dinner."

Tolliver walked around the table and took hold of her wrist. He held it tightly—so tightly that she bit her lip.

"But let's not forget who rules in this house, Amanda," he said to her. "When we have guests, they'll be invited by me. Men and women who can do us some good. Is that understood?"

"Y-Yes."

"Are you sure?"

"Yes, I'm sure."

He smiled and released her wrist.

"That's good," he said. "I'll go and change for our guest now."

As he left, she continued to fuss with the table, determined not to rub her wrist.

THIRTY-SIX

The cab stopped in front of the large two-story home on Telegraph Hill. Clint stepped down and paid the driver.

"I don't envy you, mister," the man said.

"Why not?"

"Do you know who lives there?"

"I do," Clint said. "I'm here to have dinner."

"With them?"

"What's wrong with them?"

"That's the Tolliver house. She ain't bad. Kinda stuck up, but real pretty."

"And him?"

"Well, he's a bastard, pure and simple," the driver said. "Whatever you're lookin' to get from him, you ain't gonna get it."

"I guess I'll have to find out for myself."

"You gonna be goin' back to the hotel after dinner?" the man asked.

"I am."

"I'll come back for you. Tell me what time."

"Dinner's at seven," Clint said. "Come back at ten, I'd appreciate it."

"Sure," the man said. "I'll be curious to hear what happened, if that's all right."

"Don't see anything wrong with that," Clint said. "Thanks for the ride."

"Good luck to you."

The cab drove off and Clint approached the front door. He knocked, and was surprised when the door was opened by Max, the bodyguard.

"Hello, Max."

"You think you're smart," Max said.

"About what?"

"You got Hawkins fired."

"Did he get fired?" Clint asked. "Pity. But why is that my fault?"

"Don't think I don't know," Max said. "Come this way."

Clint entered the house and closed the door behind him. There was a large grandfather clock in the hall that said it was ten minutes to seven.

He followed Max down a hall.

"Where are we going?" he asked.

"The boss wants to see you before dinner," Max said. "In his office."

"Okay."

He followed Max the rest of the way in silence. When they came to a wide doorway, Max stepped aside and said, "You can go in."

"Thanks."

Max eyed him coldly as he stepped past him.

"Come in, sir," a man behind a large cherry wood desk said.

He was sixty, maybe more, but an imposing-looking man nevertheless. Broad-shouldered and deep-chested, with a mane of gray hair. He stood behind his desk, but held out his hand. Clint had to go to him to shake. It was a power play right from the beginning.

Clint shook his hand.

"Have a seat, Mr. Adams. I am Ben Tolliver."

"Yes, sir, I figured that out."

Tolliver sat behind his desk.

"I won't offer you anything since we're about to have dinner, but I thought we should chat for a few minutes before that."

"Fine."

Tolliver sat back in his chair.

"My wife tells me you think her life is in danger," he said. "That you have some sort of . . . death list."

"It's not my list, but it was sent to me."

"May I see it?"

"Of course."

Clint took it from his pocket, leaned forward, and held it out to Tolliver—but not far enough. The man had to sit forward to reach it. Two could play power games, no matter how childish they might be.

Tolliver unfolded the list and read it.

"I know all these people."

"Your wife said she recognized the names. People you've done business with in the past?"

Tolliver dropped the list on Clint's side of the desk. Clint left it there.

"Yes, I've done business with these nine men sometime over the course of the past ten years. I don't know why my wife's name would be on such a list."

"Do you know anyone who would want to harm your wife?" Clint asked.

"Harm her, no," the man said. "But harm me by harming her, of course."

"And who would that be?"

"A man in my position doesn't get where he is without making enemies, Mr. Adams," Tolliver said almost proudly.

"I understand," Clint said, "but would you have any specific names?"

"Many names," Tolliver said. "Men—and women—who are waiting for me to trip and fall. You must experience the same thing, a man of your reputation."

"Yes," Clint said, "it would be hard for me to make a complete list."

"So there, you understand."

"Mr. Tolliver, I just want you to know that I'm available to protect your wife—"

"Just between you and me, Adams," Tolliver said, "I am very capable of protecting my wife. I suggest we go into the dining room and have dinner. When we're done, I'll thank you for your help, but it really won't be necessary."

Clint had two thoughts. The first was to get up and leave. The second was to eat the man's food and listen at the table for anything that might be helpful.

Ben Tolliver was either very confident in his ability protect his wife, or he didn't want her protected at all. If that was the case, there was a strong chance that he had something to do with makeup of that list, if he hadn't written it out himself.

THIRTY-SEVEN

When Tolliver walked Clint into the dining room, Amanda looked surprised.

"You're here!" she said to Clint.

"Yes," Clint said, "Max was nice enough to introduce me to your husband as soon as I arrived."

She gave her husband a long look. Max was standing at the door of the room with his hands folded in front of him.

"We're ready for dinner, my love," Tolliver said. "Why don't you tell our guest where you'd like him to sit?"

Tolliver sat at the head of the table. With his wife sitting at his left, she asked Clint to sit at the man's right, directly across from her.

"Oh, Amanda," Tolliver said before they all actually sat, "I neglected to tell you we'll be having another guest for dinner."

She stared at him.

"Oh? Who?"

"A friend of mine," Tolliver said. He looked at Clint. "I hope you don't mind?"

"It's not my place to mind," Clint said. "It's your home."

"Exactly," Tolliver said. "My dear? Another place setting?"

At that point there was a knock at the door.

"Max?" Tolliver said.

"Yes, sir."

Amanda gave Clint a helpless look. Rather than be seated, they all waited for the fourth member of their dinner party.

Max reappeared, leading a well-dressed man in his early forties. Not only was he well dressed, but Clint noticed he was well heeled, wearing a well-oiled holster with a well-cared-for Colt in it.

"Ah, Perry," Tolliver said, "glad you could make it."

"I appreciated the invitation, Mr. Tolliver," the man said.

"May I present my wife, Amanda?"

"Ma'am," the man said with a slight bow.

"And this is our other dinner guest, Mr. Clint Adams. This is my good friend Perry Silver," Tolliver said.

"Adams," the man said. "I've heard of you."

Clint inclined his head and said, "I've heard nothing of you."

Silver smiled.

"That suits me just fine."

"Shall we sit and eat?" Tolliver asked.

Clint thought the man looked incredibly pleased with himself.

And the attitude increased all through dinner.

* * *

It was never made clear throughout the meal how Ben Tolliver knew Silver, or what it was that Perry Silver did for a living. The conversation, rather than being helpful, was hopelessly innocuous.

Amanda kept looking across the table at Clint, and he could see that she was worried. Her husband was acting as if Clint's death list did not even exist.

After dinner Tolliver invited the men into the study for some brandy. Clint agreed, thinking perhaps something would be said once they were out of Amanda's earshot.

In the study, with brandy snifters in their hands, Tolliver got to the point.

"Adams, I want you to know that Perry here will be taking over the job of my wife's security. He's not only replacing Hawkins, but Max will be working directly under his supervision."

"I see."

"It's what I do," Silver said to Clint. "I . . . take care of people."

"Taking care of people" had more than one meaning to Clint.

"So you see," Tolliver said, "while I appreciate your offer to protect her, I have everything covered." He indicated Perry Silver. "I have the best money can buy."

"I'm sure you do," Clint said.

Tolliver put his brandy snifter down and gave Clint a long look.

"I'd appreciate it, from, this point forward, if you would not see or speak to my wife again. I hope you understand."

"I understand the words," Clint said.

"That's all I need," Tolliver said. He looked at the big bodyguard standing by the door. "Max? Would you show Mr. Adams to the door?"

"Yes, sir. With pleasure."

As Clint started for the door, Perry Silver stepped into his path.

"Don't get it my way, Adams," Silver said.

"I'll make a note," Clint said, and stepped past him.

When Max slammed the door behind him, Clint hesitated. The cab had not yet arrived. He wondered if there was some way to get back inside to see Amanda before he left when he heard a whispered voice call to him urgently.

"Clint! Over here!"

He tried to see in the dark, finally saw her standing against the wall to the right, in the shadows, away from any of the windows. He joined her in the shadows.

"I wanted to see you before you left, but I knew Ben wouldn't let me."

"He's warned me off," Clint said. "Apparently he's putting a lot of confidence in this fella Perry Silver. He doesn't want me anywhere near you."

"I don't know who he is," she whispered, pulling her shawl tightly around her as if she was chilled to the bone. "I've never seen him or heard of him."

"Neither have I," he said.

"I don't know what to do," she said. "Are you—I mean, will you do what my husband asks?"

"Amanda, if it's okay with you, I'm going to do what I can to keep you alive and well."

She seemed relieved by that.

"Do you think—I mean, it isn't possible that my husband . . . that Ben has something to do with that list?" she asked.

"Amanda, you're the one who's going to have to decide if he has a reason to want you dead."

"I can't—I don't know—"

"If you think of something," he said, "you know where I am. What will your days be like?"

She shrugged.

"I stay home, I shop, at night I go out to the casinos."

"Okay," Clint said, "the casinos. That's where we can see each other."

"If he still lets me go," she said. "And if he does, I'll probably have Max and that man, Silver, with me."

"We'll deal with that when the time comes," Clint said.

Suddenly, his cab appeared in front of the house.

"Now who can that be?" she asked fearfully.

"That's for me," he said. He touched her arm. "I'll see you soon."

"I hope so," she said.

"Don't doubt it," he told her, and headed for the cab.

THIRTY-EIGHT

Clint walked into the lobby of the Lucky Strike, thinking about his next move. The clerk with the attitude who checked him in was behind the desk.

Clint approached the desk and the man flinched, as if he thought Clint was coming to hit him.

"Where's your boss?" he asked.

"Um, he's in the casino."

"Any messages for me? Telegrams? Anything?" Clint asked.

"No, sir."

"Okay," he said. "If anything comes in—oh, never mind." There would be no telegrams this late at night. "Thanks."

"Yes, sir."

Clint turned, walked across the lobby, eyed the entrance to the saloon and the entrance to the casino. And made his choice.

He entered the casino.

* * *

Dirker was dressed in a tuxedo and walking the room. He stopped and hovered near the blackjack tables, and then the poker tables.

"Miss it?"

He turned and saw Clint.

"Miss what? Playing poker?" Dirker asked.

Clint nodded.

"Yeah, sometimes."

"You could still play in private games," Clint said.

"No," Dirker said, "once I give in, I don't think I'd be able to stop. I'll just have to settle for being the house and raking it in. Just get back?"

"Yup."

"Anything interesting happen?"

"Oh, yeah."

Dirker looked around. There were people all around them.

"Let's go someplace quiet."

"The bar?" Clint asked.

"No," Dirker said. "My office. Follow me."

He led Clint to the back of the casino in through a doorway into a small office.

"I keep two offices, this one, and one in the hotel. Have a seat and fill me in."

They sat across from each other and Clint told Dirker about the dinner.

"Perry Silver?" Dirker asked. "I never heard of him."

"I'll check with Rick Hartman in the morning," Clint said. "Even if he doesn't know who he is, he'll find out. And I'll send a telegram to Talbot Roper with his description."

"You think this guy's the killer?"

"He's very calm," Clint said. "I wouldn't put killing past him."

"Why would he send you that list?"

"You're a smart guy," Clint said.

"I am?"

"Well," Clint said, "you have the analytical mind of a killer. You tell me."

Dirker took a moment, then said, "He wanted to try you."

"Lots of people like to try me."

"Yeah, but not in the street," Dirker said. "He got a kick outta sending you ridin' all over the country. He woulda loved it if he could've killed all ten people while you were doing that. But you outsmarted him, and came here. Now he's here, too, to finish it."

Clint stared at his friend.

"That's possible," Clint said. "Tolliver hired him, though."

"What makes you say that?"

"I don't think he'd have a reason to come up with this plan on his own," Clint said. "I mean, we've never met. There's no vengeance here."

"So Tolliver hires him to kill all these men all over the country. And then to kill his wife. Why?"

"Don't know."

"How are you gonna find out?"

"Don't know that either," Clint said. "Yet."

He stood up.

"Where are you goin'?"

"I'm going to get a beer, do some thinking, then go to my room. I'll write some telegrams so I can just send them in the morning."

"Want me to have somebody do that for you?"

"No," Clint said, "I'll do it myself."

"Well, I'll be here 'til late, if you wanna talk later," Dirker said.

"Okay, King," Clint said. "Thanks."

"For what?"

"For giving me the benefit of your devious mind."

THIRTY-NINE

In the morning Clint was awakened by knocking at his door. He padded from the bedroom to the front room and answered the door.

He opened the door and found a bellman standing in the hall.

"Mr. Adams?"

"That's right."

"I was told to give these to you, sir."

Clint saw that the young man was holding telegrams in his hand.

"Thanks," he said, accepting them.

He closed the door, put the gun down on a nearby table, and read the telegrams.

Later he found Dirker in the lobby, and they went into the dining room for breakfast together.

"You sent the bellman up with those telegrams?" he asked.

"I did."

"Did you read them?"

"Only the one from my guy, because it came to me first."

"Well, the one from your guy says the same thing as the one from Talbot Roper."

"The four men left on that list all came up with the same name."

Clint nodded.

"Ben Tolliver as the only man they know who'd try to have them killed."

"But why?" Dirker asked.

"I don't think I need to know why," Clint said. "I think the list is Tolliver's, and the gunman is Perry Silver."

"Well, Silver is here in San Francisco," Dirker said. "I guess that means those four are safe?"

"Unless Tolliver—or Silver—has somebody else to send after them," Clint said. "Tolliver certainly has the money to hire a killer in each place. I'll send telegrams back that the men are to continue to be covered."

"I can send my man that telegram."

"I'm going to the office, so I'll just have a reply sent. You have your own work to do."

"What else are you gonna do today?"

"I'm still going to send a telegram to Rick Hartman. I'm going to see what I can find out from both him and Roper about Perry Silver. I need to know who I'm dealing with."

The waiter came with their steak and eggs. This time Clint consumed the whole meal before it could get cold.

As they walked out into the lobby, Dirker asked, "Have you thought about getting Amanda Tolliver out of that house?"

"I have," Clint said. "I don't think Tolliver would have her killed in his own home, though. Too many questions."

"Well, if you do decide to get her out of there, you can always bring her here. We'll make her very comfortable in the hotel."

"I appreciate that, King," Clint said. "I'll let you know what I decide."

"Do you think you have that much time?" Dirker asked. "If she goes to the casinos tonight with her body-guards, Silver might decide to go ahead and do the job."

"But Max will be with them," Clint said, "and if I'm any judge of people, the big bodyguard is in love with the lady."

"Really?"

"Looks at her like a lovesick puppy. Silver's going to have to deal with Max before he can dispose of Amanda. But don't worry, I'll be in Portsmouth Square tonight."

"If you need me," Dirker said, "you know where to find me."

"I know," Clint said, and left.

He stopped at the telegraph office, replied to the tele-grams he had, then sent a couple of his own. He sent the same question to both Rick and Roper: Who is Perry Silver?

After that he decided to do some research of his own. He went to the offices of the *San Francisco Chronicle* and spent some time in their morgue looking for any mention of Perry Silver.

He didn't find any, but there were a few stories about opponents of Ben Tolliver who'd showed up dead. There was no mention, however, in any of those cases, about Tolliver ever being questioned by the police.

So it appeared Ben Tolliver was protected.

No surprise.

FORTY

Clint got dressed for Portsmouth Square.

He'd reviewed his options during the course of the day, and decided to get Amanda Tolliver out of the line of fire before anything else happened. He'd take Dirker up on his offer of a room for her. Once that was done, he could deal with Perry Silver.

During the course of the day he'd received the replies from his telegrams. Rick Hartman and Talbot Roper gave him the same information. Perry Silver was a killer for hire—a high-priced one. But there was nothing in his background that matched this death list thing. This was totally different.

He left his room, went down to the lobby. He hadn't told Amanda which casino to meet him in, but he felt sure he'd find her at the Alhambra again. She struck him as a smart woman. May not have been the smartest thing in the world to marry Ben Tolliver, but on the other hand, she'd only been nineteen at the time.

He didn't see Dirker on the way out, didn't look for

him. Out front he had the doorman get him a cab, and
told the driver to take him to the Alhambra.

He spent a couple of hours in the casino, played a few
hands of blackjack—a game he didn't really like—spent
some time at the bar. He didn't bother getting involved
in a poker game. That required a longer commitment,
and he didn't have the time to spend.

Finally, Amanda appeared. Perry Silver came in
ahead of her, Max was right behind her, both of them
dressed all in black. She was dressed in a long blue gown,
had a shawl on over bare shoulders and generous cleav-
age. She came down the steps, her eyes sweeping the
room. Clint was right there in her line of sight, but she
gave no indication that she saw him. She did, though. He
was sure of that.

He watched her as she walked around the room. Max
kept his eyes on her, but Silver watched the whole room.
Clint was sure the killer—and he was sure Perry Silver
was a killer—had seen him.

Clint was curious—curious enough to ask some questions. He decided the direct approach was the best way
to go. So he walked across the room to where Amanda
was playing some faro. Max was standing right behind
her, but Silver was off to the side of the table.

"Buy you a drink?" he asked Perry.

Silver looked at him without surprise.

"Why not?"

He tapped Max on the shoulder, told him where he
was going. The big man reacted with a careless shrug—
the kind that said he couldn't care less.

Perry followed Clint to the bar. The killer had no holster on his hip today, but Clint could see the bulge beneath the man's jacket. He was wearing a shoulder rig.

"What'll you have?" he asked.

"Beer."

"Two beers," Clint told the bartender.

When the bartender put them on the bar, Clint picked one up and handed it to Silver. At the same time he handed him the list. Then he looked over at the faro table, saw that Amanda was looking at them over her shoulder.

"What's this?" Silver asked.

"I thought you'd like that back."

Silver looked at the list.

"Five names are crossed off."

"You know why."

Silver didn't respond, he just looked back at the list.

"What about these other four?"

"Oh, they're safe."

"Are they?"

"Oh, yes," Clint said. "I made sure of that. They're safe."

Silver looked at Clint, sipped his beer, then smiled and put the list away in his pocket. He turned his attention back to his half-finished beer.

"Why the list, Perry?" Clint asked. "I know what you do for a living, but that kind of game has never been in your background. Killing nine men, that was an easy job for you. Especially shooting them in the back. But why send me the list?"

Silver studied Clint for a few moments, and Clint thought he'd lie.

Instead he said, "Boredom."

"Murder for hire started to bore you?"

"You can get bored with anything," Silver said. He looked across the floor at Amanda. "Even a beautiful woman."

"Is that why Amanda is on your list?" Clint asked. "Because her husband is bored with her?"

"You'd have to ask him why she's on the list," Silver said. "I don't ask why. Knowing why is not part of my job." He put the mug down on the bar. "Thanks for the beer, and the chat."

"Max is not just going to let you kill her, you know," Clint said.

"Max won't be a problem."

"I'm not just going to stand by and watch you kill her either."

Silver grinned.

"Well, you might be a problem," he said, "but it's one I can handle."

"Are you sure?"

"Dead sure," Silver said, "or I never would have sent you that note."

"Well, then, maybe you and me, we should settle it," Clint said. "That is, before you kill her."

"No, I don't think so," Silver said. "Money first, then fun. Again, thanks for the beer."

Silver walked away from the bar, back to the faro table.

FORTY-ONE

Amanda—probably confused about what was to happen—finally decided to play poker. That put her at a table with five men, in full view of the entire casino.

Clint walked over to the table. Once again Max was standing right behind her, and Silver was off to one side of the table, watching the people.

Clint sidled up next to Max and said, "How about taking a little break, Max. Buy you a beer?"

Max turned his head and gave Clint a cold look.

"Come on," Clint said. "I've got something to tell you. I think you'll find it interesting."

Max turned his head back to the table.

"Come on, Max," Clint said. "It has to do with Amanda."

Max gave him another look, this one with a flicker of interest in his eyes.

"Come on," Clint said. "Silver took a break. Now you take one."

Max looked over at Silver, then back at Clint. Finally, he leaned over and said something to Amanda.

"Fine," Clint heard her say, "go."

Max walked over to Silver and said something to him. Silver laughed. As Clint and Max walked to the bar, Silver stood behind Amanda. It would have been very easy for him to kill her if there hadn't been all those other people in the room.

At the bar Clint didn't bother to ask Max what he'd have. He just ordered two beers. When he handed one to Max, he handed him the two telegrams he'd received, identifying Perry Silver as a killer for hire. Max frowned, read both telegrams. Clint was glad he was able to read.

"What's this mean?" he demanded.

"It means your friend Silver over there hasn't been hired to protect Amanda. He's been hired to kill her."

Clint didn't bother trying to explain to Max about the list. It was enough to let him know that Amanda was in danger.

"But . . . w-who?"

"Who do you think?"

Max stared at him without comprehension.

Oh boy, Clint thought. This is going to be harder than I thought.

"Max, Perry works for the same man you work for."

"But . . . why would Mr. Tolliver hire him to kill Mrs. Tolliver?"

"I don't know," Clint said. "Does that matter? Look across the room. He could kill her real easy, standing behind her like that."

Max took a quick step away from the bar, but Clint stopped him.

"He won't do it, not in front of all these people."

Max stepped back.

"What do I do?"

"Well, you could kill him before he kills her."

Max stared at Clint, his eyes wide, and suddenly he looked more like a scared boy than a bodyguard.

"I ain't never killed nobody," he said. "I broke some bones, yeah, but . . . I ain't no killer."

"Well, that's okay, Max," Clint said. "There's something else you can do."

"What's that?"

"Just help me get her away from him."

"And then what?"

"Then we take her someplace safe."

"Won't they look for her?"

"Probably," Clint said, "but I'll handle that. You help me get her someplace safe, and then you stay with her. I'll handle the rest."

Max looked over at Amanda, with Silver standing behind her.

"Okay," he said.

"Good."

"I'm sorry about . . . the other thing."

"Hey, Max," Clint said, "not everybody can kill, you know?"

"Yeah," Max said. "Yeah, I know."

"Okay," Clint said, "now this is what we'll do . . ."

Max listened while Clint outlined his plan. He didn't say a word until Clint was done.

"You got all that?" Clint asked.

"I got it."

"Okay," Clint said, "you go back to the poker table."

"What do I tell Mrs. Tolliver?"

"Don't worry," Clint said. "She'll be ready for whatever happens."

Max thought about that, then nodded and said, "Okay."

He started away from the bar, then stopped and looked at Clint.

"Mr. Adams, this is on the level, right?"

"Yeah, Max, it's on the level."

"'cause if it ain't . . ."

"I know," Clint said. "You won't kill me, but you'll break something."

FORTY-TWO

Clint remained at the bar while Amanda played. On two occasions she looked at him over her shoulder. Both times he just nodded.

Finally, she called it quits and cashed out. They gave her the money she had won, and she put it in her purse and stood up. She turned and said something to Max. He said something back. Perry Silver was too far away to hear what was being said.

They started for the door and Clint moved to intercept them.

"Hello, Amanda," he said.

She stopped.

"Clint, hello."

"Have a good night?"

"Very good."

Max put his hand against Clint's chest and pushed him back.

"I told you to stay away!" he snapped.

"Come on, buddy. I bought you a beer."

Max poked him in the chest with his forefinger.

"Stay away."

Amanda started for the door, and Max followed. Clint made to follow them, but Perry Silver stepped in his way.

"Listen to the big guy," he advised.

"Oh, sure," Clint said, "sure, I'll listen to him. I wouldn't want to get Max mad."

"You don't have to worry about Max, Adams," Silver said. "You only have to worry about me."

"Sure, Perry, sure," Clint said. "I'll worry about you."

Silver started for the door, and Clint stopped him.

"How about another drink?"

"Sorry," Silver said. "The lady is ready to go home, and her husband is waiting."

"Well," Clint said, "I wouldn't want to keep a husband waiting."

Silver nodded to him, then turned and went out the door.

Clint stopped one of the girls who was carrying drinks from the bar and asked, "Is there another way out of here?"

"Sure," she said. "Follow me."

He did. She took him to a side entrance, then gave him a pretty smile.

"You want my address?" she asked. "You could wait there for me."

He smiled back and said, "Another time maybe. Thanks."

FORTY-THREE

Clint went to the Lucky Strike and met Max in the lobby.

"Where is she?" Clint asked.

"Your friend, he took her to a room."

"Come on," Clint said, "let's go."

Max led the way up the stairs to Amanda's room. Clint knocked on the door. She answered and let them in, then threw herself into his arms.

"Thank you."

"Sure, Amanda."

She backed away from him and touched Max on the arm. He just nodded and stared at her in a lovesick way.

"Now what?" she asked.

"Well," Clint said, "Silver will go to your husband and tell him what happened."

"Ben will fire him."

"It won't be as easy to fire Silver as it was to fire Hawkins. No, they'll come looking for you."

"But . . . where will they look?" she asked.

"I don't know," Clint said.

"Here?" Max asked.

Clint looked at Max.

"I hope not."

It dawned on him then that while he was doing research on Perry Silver during the day, maybe Silver was doing the same on him. But Clint had quite a few acquaintances in San Francisco, and a few friends. How would they pick out King Dirker?

There was a knock on the door.

"Who is it?" Clint asked.

"Desk clerk, Mr. Adams."

Clint pulled his gun, waved Amanda and Max away from the door, then opened it. It was Lou, the older desk clerk.

"What is it, Lou?"

"Fella downstairs told me to tell you he's waitin' down there for you."

"What fella?"

"Said his name was Silver."

"Where's the boss?"

"He's with that fella," Lou said. "Somethin' ain't right, Mr. Adams. He also told me to give you this."

Lou held out a slip of paper. Clint took it, and saw that it was the list. The list of ten names. Only now there was eleven.

The name on the end was Kenneth Dirker.

FORTY-FOUR

Clint told Max to stay with Amanda.

"What are you going to do?" Amanda asked.

"Save my friend."

He went down to the lobby with Lou.

"Where were they?"

"Here," Lou said. "Behind the desk."

"King said he had two offices, one here in the hotel."

"That's right."

"Take me to the hotel office."

"This way."

Lou led Clint to an office behind the desk area. The door was closed.

"All right," Clint said. "Go back out front."

The desk clerk left and Clint put his hand on the door-knob. The door wasn't locked. He opened it and stepped in. The woman sitting behind the desk looked at him and smiled.

"Wendy, isn't it?" he asked.

"You remembered," said the girl he had last seen in Roper's office.

"Are you Silver's partner?"

"Perry doesn't have partners," she said. "He uses people."

"And he's using you?"

"Yes."

"And you don't mind?"

She shrugged. "He pays for the privilege."

"So what do you do?"

"Me? I do research."

"Is that what you were doing at Roper's office?"

"Yes."

"And you did the research here? And found out about this place?"

"Several places," she said. "Perry said you'd pick this one."

"And now you're here to . . . what? Give me directions?"

"He'll trade your friend for the woman."

"I can't do that. He'll kill her."

"If you don't, he'll kill your friend."

"That may be," Clint said, "but I can't just hand over the woman."

"Just give her back to her husband."

"Same thing. She'll still end up dead."

Wendy stood up. Suddenly, she looked frightened.

"You're afraid he'll kill you if you fail here."

"If he does," she said, "you'll be responsible for my death."

"Where is he?"

"I don't know."

"Then where am I supposed to take Amanda, and make the exchange?"

She handed him a piece of paper. On it was an address.

"This is on the Barbary Coast."

"Yes."

"That would give him the advantage," Clint said. "He can buy help there for a dollar a man."

"Then you won't go?"

"No."

She seemed confused.

"So what now?" he asked.

"I—I don't know."

"Well, go to him and tell him I won't trade."

"I can't. I don't know—I can't."

"You work for him. You must know where he is, how to contact him."

She didn't answer.

"Did he go back to the Tolliver house?"

"I told you, I don't know."

If she was simply lying, he didn't think she would have been so nervous. Maybe she really didn't know.

"Okay, then leave," he said. "Just leave. I'll find him myself."

She walked to the door, then stopped.

"What's wrong? Go out the door."

"I can't," she said.

"Why not?"

She turned to face him.

"He said if I come out the door without you, he'll kill me."

"So then he's not on the Barbary Coast," Clint said. "He's still in the building."

"I can't leave this room."

"All right," he said. "Stay. I'll leave."

He started for the door. She stepped in his way.

"If you kill him . . ."

"What?"

"I'll be . . . grateful." She put her hand on his hip, then moved it to his crotch. He grabbed her hand and pushed it away.

"You can be grateful in other ways," he said. "There's no need for that."

He started for the door again, then stopped.

"If you want him dead, where is he?"

"I would tell you if I could."

He nodded, said, "Stay here," and went out the door.

FORTY-FIVE

When he reached the lobby, he saw Lou lying on the floor behind the desk. The lobby itself was empty. Except for two men. King Dirker was there, with Perry Silver standing behind him with his gun in his hand.

Clint leaned over long enough to determine that Lou was alive.

"Come out from behind the desk," Silver said.

Clint did so.

"Where's the girl?"

"Wendy? She's in the office. Waiting for me to kill you."

Silver laughed.

"Your best days are behind you, Adams," he said.

"Jesus," Dirker said, "just do it, Clint."

"He can't," Silver said. "He's not even wearing a gun."

"Well, give him one," Dirker said, "then you'll see."

"Shut up!" Silver said.

Clint reached behind his back for his .25.

"Get the woman," Silver said, "and bring her down."

"And then what?"

"I'll do my job."

"What Tolliver paid you to do?"

"Yes."

"But why?" Clint asked. "Why did he pay you to kill all those people?"

"I told you, I don't care," Silver said. "I'll just do my job."

"Well," Clint said, "you'll have to kill me to get to Amanda, or to any of the rest of your death list."

"Kill you?"

"What's wrong?" Clint asked. "Can't kill unless you're being paid?"

"Oh, I'll get paid," Silver said. "You're in my way. Tolliver will pay me to remove you."

"Then try it."

"You're a fool."

Clint had hit targets as small as a two-bit piece. Even smaller. Silver was standing with King Dirker in front of him as a shield, but his head was visible over Dirker's shoulder. With his modified Colt, this would have been an easy shot.

"All right," Silver said. "I don't have much choice. Killing the Gunsmith will be good for my rep anyway."

Clint was hoping Silver would step out from behind Dirker to take his shot, but he didn't. He stayed where he was and extended his right arm.

Clint drew and fired.

Amanda and Max were in the saloon, sitting at a table. He had a beer, she a glass of brandy. They were waiting for the law to arrive. It would be up to the authorities to deal with Ben Tolliver. King Dirker had heard everything Silver had said about working for Tolliver before Clint shot him in the forehead with his .25.

In the morning Clint would send telegrams telling the other four men on the list that they were safe.

Clint and Dirker were standing at the bar.

"What about the girl?" Dirker asked.

"Wendy? I let her go. She was just afraid of Silver."

"You know, that was kind of close," Dirker said, taking a long pull on his beer.

"Why didn't you just step aside?"

"Are you kiddin'?" Dirker said. "I didn't want to distract you. I knew you only had that little twenty-five on you."

"I told you it would do the job," Clint said.

"Yeah, you did," Dirker said. "And it did the job—but only because it was in your hands."

Watch for

THE VICAR OF ST. JAMES

364th novel in the exciting GUNSMITH series
from Jove

Coming in April!

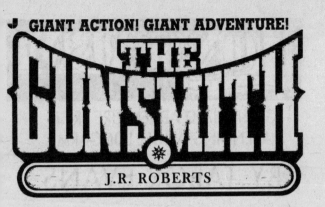

GIANT ACTION! GIANT ADVENTURE!

THE Gunsmith

J.R. ROBERTS

GIANT-SIZED ADVENTURE FROM AVENGING ANGEL LONGARM.

BY TABOR EVANS

penguin.com/actionwesterns

DON'T MISS A YEAR OF

Slocum Giant
by
Jake Logan

Slocum Giant 2004:
Slocum in the Secret
Service

Slocum Giant 2005:
Slocum and the Larcenous
Lady

Slocum Giant 2006:
Slocum and the Hanging
Horse

Slocum Giant 2007:
Slocum and the Celestial
Bones

Slocum Giant 2008:
Slocum and the Town
Killers

Slocum Giant 2009:
Slocum's Great
Race

Slocum Giant 2010:
Slocum Along
Rotten Row

penguin.com/actionwesterns

7-10

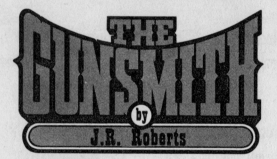